LEVI SWEENEY

Songbird!

A Collection of Poems and Stories

First published by Blue Candle Holdings, LLC 2025

First edition

ISBN: 979-8-218-69758-7

This book was professionally typeset on Reedsy.
Find out more at reedsy.com

To Bill Hoke.

"If I find in myself a desire which no experience in this world can satisfy, the most probable explanation is that I was made for another world."

C.S. LEWIS

Contents

III   Bird Song

I

Bird Seed

These are from my "consciously poetic" phase. These are not great poems, not all of them, but I am proud of them all, even in hindsight. I was first trying to be a poet when I wrote these.

1

The Elder

He has a heart of gold, head like an egg
  To the Father Above, I daily beg
  He who is full of years, full of much good
  May he come to himself in a dark wood.
  But his mind is muddled, his eyes are dim
  Can he still make the choice to follow Him?

He who lived a life of peace, hope, and love
  Can he still put his faith in Him Above?
  But He who reigns above is no doubt just
  He saw the end when all was merely dust
  The mind of Him who reigns cannot be known
  The hearts of all men seen by Him alone.

His word pierces into the souls of all
  After all men he sends a type of call
  This old man whom I love with all my heart
  I pray for his soul when it does depart
  That his soul will go find eternal rest

That his soul will pass the eternal test
For on the day when he does breathe his last
Into darkness may his soul not be cast
Instead may he have ears, that he may hear
That thanks to the Lion, he need not fear.

For the Lion saves all who trust in Him
Even those whose senses have gone dim.
The Elder's final days have come not yet
I pray that he will have naught to regret.
I pray that should he find himself alone
It will not be before the Great White Throne.

Some tell of a place which is not so rough
For those whose souls are simply good enough.
If the elder cannot reach the pearly gates
May he not find himself in dire straights
May the Elder go to his realm most still
May his soul be saved by the Lion's will.

But the Lion's will is not always clear
Perhaps the Elder will be judged severe
For infractions secret or on display
Known to none but him before such a day
If he has such sins may he fast atone
And not be found before the Great White Throne.

But the Elder the Lion may still yet save
For the Elder is not yet near the grave.
Though his mind is clouded and his speech slow
The Great Lion he still may come to know.

2

The Cat and the Rats

When the cat did leave and go far away
　　The rats did emerge from their holes and say
　　"What have we to do with stately affairs?
　　Let us chew and gnaw and forget our cares!
　　Shall we not taste the flesh of man and mouse?
　　Shall we not eat all that is in this house?
　　For rightly do we deserve all we want!
　　Without the cat the world is our font!"

And so the rats did come upon the hearth
　　And devoured all they could with much mirth
　　But when there was naught left to eat and chew
　　The rats said, "Let us make this house anew!
　　It will be a rathole like no other!
　　Full of glory, with each rat a brother!
　　With no cat to stand in our way to joy
　　We will be safe from those who would destroy!
　　Now let us break this house down to dust
　　And build it back up in our image just!"

And so they gnawed the house down into grime
   Until there was naught left but muddled slime.
   And when the rats had made the house no more
   They said, "Oh woe! What did we do that for?
   For the ground is hard and the rain is cold.
   The house was not like that in days of old.
   Our hands and minds are not made for the job
   Of making a home for this lonely mob.
   Oh cat, though harm you did give us indeed
   You only harmed when we caused yours to bleed.
   We see stupidly, shockingly too late
   That our greed has consigned us to this fate."

And just when all the rats had lost all hope
   A golden light came up from yonder slope.
   A peaceful, joyful warmth engulfed them all
   Sweet music came forth like a songbird's call.
   Just who had come over that grassy hill?
   It was the cat! But he came not to kill.

"Fear not!" the noble cat did kindly say.
   "Come, let us not be enemies today.
   For though we once did fight tooth and nail
   Now I bring a love which will not fail.
   My gracious master for whom I do speak
   Has sent me to protect the humble meek.
   He has prepared a home for those who stand
   For virtue, courage, and all goodness grand.
   He is the truth, and welcomes all who vow
   To love what's good, and not to evil bow.
   His house is one of order, that is true.

But upon order joy shall fast accrue.
But entrance to this house comes with a fee.
Fear not. This payment shall be paid by me."

Then something happened which the rats saw not:
The cat became a rat, and smelled of rot.
But though his fur and face were black as coal
His golden eyes betrayed a golden soul.
"It is I!" the Cat-Rat said, "I am here!
Follow me, and you will find all that's dear."

But the wretched rats, they saw not at all.
Instead, the Cat-Rat, they did rend and maul.
The Cat-Rat said, "You rats, why must this be?"
The rats did reply, "What? Do you not see?
We don't want a second home, just the first!
This light vision you proclaim masks the worst!
What good ever came of a rat that sings
Of a new house where his kind rules all things?
Was it not enough when we lived in holes
Where we stole sweet crumbs and did sup with moles?
Our greed for all we wanted was not checked
Which led to our old home becoming wrecked.
So let us wait for the Cat to return.
As for your new tidings, they we do spurn."

The Cat-Rat told them that he was the Cat
But they did not see; they saw just a rat.
They hanged him high on an accursed tree
But some came to mourn him, one or two or three.
But when the Cat-Rat was laid in the ground

The heart of the world did greatly pound.
Then he, the Cat-Rat, did from his grave rise
Full of glory beyond all mortal eyes.
Some few rats, who had listened to him speak
Saw that thanks to him, things need not be bleak.
The Cat-Rat told his followers, few but fit
That on his Master's throne, he must now sit.
But he promised that he would come again
And take all the righteous into his den.

"Each of you rats was once but a foul pest,"
The Cat-Rat said, "but come the final test
If you stand with me and my master one
With your sooty coating you will be done
Just as it was in days in the past far
When no single rat had a single mar
You I will cleanse with a fiery fount
And be made as pure as a snowy mount
And then the house for which you greatly yearn
By loyalty, this you indeed will earn
Loyalty to the just, the right, the true
Loyalty to me, loyalty by you."

Henceforth the rats did seek to live
For him who life he came to freely give.
By faith, hope, and love to live, this they sought
For to live by such things is what all ought.
And at the end of days they gained a home
As it was written in the sacred tome.

3

Blue Candle in the Dark

He has a beard white gray and long
  As choirboys sing out their song
  He stands guilty of nothing wrong
  Oh look! A blue candle in the dark!

There is no cause to be alarmed
  Satan and friends are all disarmed
  No more shall any man be harmed
  Oh look! A blue candle in the dark!

I sought both beauty and the beast
  At the good Lord's Thanksgiving feast
  The bread of life only increased
  Oh look! A blue candle in the dark!

I dare not wear the golden ring
  Lest I be turned into machine
  It belongs only to the king
  Oh look! A blue candle in the dark!

4

Incense

Enthralls my nose in the House of the Lord
    Recruits good thoughts into my mind at once
    Devout feelings fill up my heart-of-hearts
    This smell that I detect; is it perfume?
    Wafting throughout the New Jerusalem?
    Or is it the scent of the Bread of Life Himself?

5

Father's Farewell

Good morning, creatures of our God and King
    I will soon depart my Rocky Seat.
    But the Bride I serve will still have my ring
    One last message I will repeat.

Love righteousness and hate dishonest gain
    This simple rule of life is not new.
    Whether doing so or not spares you pain
    Whether on street corner or pew.

Resist Old Nick and he will surely flee!
    So it is written and so it is.
    Without question the Truth will set you free.
    And the Truth, He is hard to miss.

6

The Sorrowful

The Courtyard
I saw a man beyond the pale
In the coldly lit dawn.
He could have fought tooth and nail
But made himself a pawn.
I wonder, in regret
What would have happened had I been bold.

The Field
I sat in gloom amid the dust
Cursed the coins in my palm.
I sold the man who was just
Like alabaster balm.
I quickly fled from my home.
Now I dwell beneath the throne of ice.

The Palace
With great pomp I celebrated
Though why I do not know.

I saw him and I prated.
I heard a rooster crow.
Here on the shores of Tarsus
I remember my glimpse of the truth.

7

Dream Country

The Hamlet
A little place
One hazy afternoon
Come a long way, long way to go
Brown-eyed, dark-haired girl
Nice little town

The Monument
A great man gone
Immortalized in steel
Through the memory of this man
Though his statue may rust
May great men come.

The Homestead
Three rooms, a loft
Older than a few trees
If the walls and the floor could speak
They would tell of young times

When small was big

The Brook
Chuckling water
Two friends walking along
This little bit of time with her
I wish it would not end
A silent heart

Thirty-One
She loves the good
She Rises early to work.
Sharp in mind, always gentle in word.
An excellent woman, who can find?
When I become excellent
She will appear.

The Road
The hamlet shrinks
As I go on my way
When I go there and back again
I will stop by this place.
She's at her door.

The City
I came near death
And it was tall and bright
A monster of steel and glass
Gleaming against the sky
It's not my home.

The Escape

My work is done
I can leave this grim place
The road goes on, and I love it.
On my way back I think
Is she still there?

The Return

This sunny place
A village by a brook
With a statue, a house, a girl
Was it just a picture?
Or is it here?

8

Spirits

The Moon
The light ruling over the nightly sky
The lady of the starry sea above
Consort of the ocean, pushing, pulling
Sister of the Earth, cousin of the Sun
Revered as a goddess in ancient days
Revered as the doorstep of heaven now
Approached through faith and song in days of old
Understood through machine and mind today.
Who is this Queen who reigns within the void?
This everlasting guardian of night?
Who placed the crown of light upon her head?
In whose name does she rule if not her own?
Of all the lords and ladies of the sky
She alone is the daughter of the King.

The Ocean
Realm of water, desert of teaming life
Terrible, mysterious, beautiful.

Black as Satan's heart, colder than his eyes
Pure as a saint, warm like an angel's kiss.
The road of the old, the wall of the new.
It threatens death to those who come to it
But gives life to those whom it approaches.
Well of life for the clever and the bold
Tomb and jail for the fool and coward.
Every corner of its face is seen
But its heart and soul hide from all who look.
Those who make their home there are safe from man
But in the great depths of the ocean sea
The law of darkest jungle reigns supreme.
Governed by the moon, neighbored by the land,
Housing life which remains unseen by all,
May there be a new sea with the new Earth.

The Sun

King of all there is, King for all of time
Hymns were sung to it, laws were made for it.
It makes the desert the domain of sin
It makes the shore of the sea a heaven.
This flaming Lord causes the slave to sweat
But the free man's fruit owes this king its life
The weary enjoy this lord's healing rays
The poet and the painter heed its call
It partners with the farmer and the rain
The author of life made it one as well.

9

Jackson

The night when they said, "The child is a boy!"
   Perish the day. At least,
   While at Abraham's feast,
   I think they thought that when I left. Was there joy?

No one will write my tombstone's epitaph
   I will not know the dog of war or puppy love
   I will not appear in a photograph
   I will not write an elegy for her I love

No one will write an elegy for me
   For I and He who loves me have eternal life.
   I pray that those who sent me off will see
   That I meant no harm to them, who took up the knife.

I will never appear on a magazine
   No one will know my name
   No fifteen-minute fame
   But I'll always hear the herald angel sing.

But those who sent me off may one day yet atone
  Those who sent for and handled that dread knife
  May they never so much as sniff the Great White Throne
  May they live out their days with gladness, joy, and life.

"All creatures of our God and King" may they proclaim
  With joy in the house of Him who loves me.
  At the Place of the Skull may they find His true name
  May they heed this: "The Truth will set you free."

He stands at the door; so wrote a wise man's pen.
  Please, please, answer the knock
  Ascend His Holy Rock
  So that I might say to you, "Hello again."

10

Jerusalem

I get off the plane at Tel Aviv,
  Is the tarmac holy ground?
  Do I hear the Lord God whispering
  When nobody is around?

For among these ancient stones and sands
  Happened much to praise and fear.
  So when you make this desert road trip
  Come on, get your soul in gear!

So was Philemon like a postcard
  Which St. Paul wrote to a friend?
  Or did St. John go see a doctor
  When he saw the world end?

Did the Crusaders stop to wonder
  When they saw the Wailing Wall?
  Or did Absalom give a stump speech
  By that old Masonic Hall?

So it's been a week, cheap hotel soap
   It is making me feel sore.
   There's soldiers on ev'ry other block
   There's talk of another war.

A holy city with streets of gold
   Would beat concrete any day.
   Let's have the peace talks at Megiddo
   Then get on our knees and pray.

On the road to Damascus
   Gonna go see something new
   Sing a psalm at Antioch
   Something beautiful and true
   Hike through Anatolia
   Take the boat over to Greece
   I've got my marching orders
   From my God, the Prince of Peace.

I'm headed home, economy class
   Thinking on the empty tomb.
   I learned so much in the holy land
   Of the fruit of Mary's womb.

Don't let this song be your only guide
   To the Good Lord's Promised Land.
   Start by looking up to Father God
   And just take his open hand.

Should I start my trip at Nazareth
   Or go straight to Calvary?

Go make a pitstop at Emmaus
And then swing by Bethany.

Take a stroll through upper Galilee
Just like those old fishermen
Then take a tour of Bethsaida
Then back to Jerusalem.

11

Clark

A mighty state within the starry sky
  A race proud and decadent, doomed to die.
  One righteous man will not escape the end,
  But his only son, far away will send.

The starry home destroyed, the son sent out
  His home is ended, there is no redoubt.
  Sent in steely basket to far-off place
  His father gambled on the human race.

Taken in by a man of the soil,
  He and his wife teach the son to toil.
  They teach their son the virtues of their land.
  They teach him for the good to firmly stand.

Mankind's yellow sun makes the boy a god,
  His little finger like an iron rod.
  When just a boy he performs mighty deeds
  Always in service to his neighbor's needs.

Now a man, he goes forth into the fray
   The son fights to keep evil ones at bay.
   Though godlike power fills his every vein,
   His one desire is that justice reign.

Never-ending battle is waged by him
   On those who commit evil on a whim.
   He knows no death, this man of starry birth
   Stories of the man, they fill up the Earth.

If he pleased, he could make himself a king
   A mighty ruler, over ev'rything.
   But to such temptations, he'd only say,
   "No. I prefer the American way."

12

The Red Mirror

"And ye shall hear of wars and rumours of wars: see that ye be not troubled: for all these things must come to pass, but the end is not yet."

These red words would not be spoken for a long time. Whether it would be four billion years or two thousand, it matters not. What does matter is that one Archangel Michael, a servant of the Man who would warn of such wars and rumors of wars, was now, at the beginning of time, afraid.

It was Heaven, and rumors of war filled the golden streets. Belial the choirmaster was preparing his battle song, and Archangel Michael, Commander of the Heavenly Host and foremost of all the angels who stood by the Lord God Yahweh, wondered. Could the coming wrath be averted? Could Belial be made to see reason? Surely someone as wise and powerful as Belial the Choirmaster could be made to see that what he planned was a thing of great folly. Surely the coming tragedy could be averted.

Michael knew what he had to do. A fraction of his power was all he needed to fashion a Red Mirror, a Red Mirror which would show many terrible things, things which God Himself knew would happen, but which Belial had the power to stop with two words: "I surrender."

Michael, armed with his Red Mirror, approached Belial. Even now, battlelines were being drawn up before the Throne itself. It was Michael's business to be there, and he went to the very edge of the lines, where Belial and his partisans stood, ready to send out their war song. Michael mourned for the loss of one third of this brother angels, one third of the starry host, seduced by the renegade choirmaster.

But Michael was prepared to make one last desperate gamble. One more ploy for peace.

Michael said,

"Brother Belial, please do not attack.
   Untold wrath and violence shall be unleashed
   Should you continue with this evil scheme.
   Look into this mirror red, please, behold.
   May you see something which will stay your hand."

Belial said,

"Brother Michael, your weak and hollow words,
   They do not move me, not one little bit.
   You have a way to see what is to come?
   Fine. I will look in your mirror red.

27

I could indeed find something worth my time."

And so Belial took the Red Mirror, and peered into it. Dark and heavy was his face.

Michael stood behind him, and knew what Belial would see: wars, plagues, crimes, all manner of evil born of sin, all manner of sin born of Belial, screaming at the devil through Michael's Red Mirror.

And Belial did look. He saw the first murder, when Cain heaved a jagged rock into the skull of Abel. He saw the Assyrians pour out the blood of their enemies like water, with the Babylonians, Persians, Greeks, and Romans doing the same.

Tyrants and warmongers weren't the only sources of fear in the Red Mirror. For every Nero, Atilla, Ivan, Robespierre, Napoleon, Hitler, Stalin, and Mao, there were a hundred ordinary murderers, ordinary adulterers, ordinary thieves, ordinary men and women who welcomed evil into their souls and let it take over their bodies and minds. Yes, some of the worst of the worst were just Tom, Dick, and Harry.

And Belial started it all.

It had all started, or all would start, when Belial said to the woman, "Ye shall not surely die. For God doth know that in the day ye eat thereof, then your eyes shall be opened, and ye shall be as gods, knowing good and evil."

And Belial put the Red Mirror down, just in time to hear from it the words:

"I am: and ye shall see the Son of man sitting on the right hand of power, and coming in the clouds of heaven."

One Belial had returned the Red Mirror to Michael, Michael said,

"Do you now see what you will bring about?
    The destruction, the death, the suffering?
    These human beings, even now on Earth,
    Who will bear this burden you are making?
    Is your heart, brother Belial, yet moved?"

And Belial, his face still dark and heavy, said in reply,

"What you have shown me, dear brother Michael,
    Is not something which makes my blood run cold.
    No, it warms my very heart to see it.
    If my rebellion will create these things,
    I welcome it with all the strength I have."

And Belial took the Red Mirror away from Michael, smashed it into pieces, and war began in Heaven.

That was the beginning, and Michael's Master would one day say of it: "I beheld Satan as lightning fall from heaven. Behold, I give unto you power to tread on serpents and scorpions, and over all the power of the enemy: and nothing shall by any means hurt you. Notwithstanding in this rejoice not, that the spirits are subject to you; but rather rejoice, because your names are written in heaven."

In the name of the Father, Son, and Holy Spirit, Amen.

13

The Child's Quest

Departure

The boy Luis sat at his mother's side
   Gripping onto her hand as she lay sick.
   Cancer had choked her body for so long
   It had been many years since she could sing.

As Luis listened to his mother speak,
   He quietly resolved to listen hard
   And do what she instructed on that day.
   The child's mother spoke the following:

"My darling boy, please listen now,
   I've only so much time.
   Make to me, please, a simple vow
   It has goodwill and rhyme.

"Please go seek God, and do not stop
   Search for Him all your life.
   Whether in park or corner shop
   Whether in peace of strife.

"Heed the Father, this I request
   In heaven and on Earth
   If this you do your very best
   Your soul will have rebirth."

The boy Luis was taken from the room
   Just barely ten years old on that sad day.
   Doctors came and went and elders whispered
   And Luis was left on the porch alone.

Luis looked at the steel gray skies above
   And he balled up his tiny fists in rage.
   He cursed the Heavens and its denizens
   And called down evil on the King of Kings.

"Why should I seek God out?" he said
   "What good is he to me?
   My mother who is almost dead
   Was almost cancer free!

"But then the tumor came again
   And now she's all but gone!
   She's Daniel in the lion's den
   And won't be safe at dawn!

"So go and rot, you King of Kings!

I care nothing for you!
You gave my mother angel's wings
Though her life's years are few!"

Luis wept on the porch, shedding hot tears
Hoping that all the Earth would share his gloom.
He did not notice, coming down the path
A plump, black-robed man of sixty-seven.

The old and kindly priest sat by his side
And hugged sad Luis as the boy kept wailing.
When Luis stopped, the priest, speaking softly
Addressed the poor boy's sorrows on that day.

"Young man," he said, "I feel your pain
I have lost loved ones too.
But know that God sends dust and rain
On all men, not on few.

"Since time began, until today,
Many have asked one thing.
Why does life toss good men away
Yet bless the evil king?

"But come with me to the old place
Where did your mother pray.
You may see Lord God's shining face!
A visit He may pay!"

Then the old priest, whose name was Father Joe,
Left the porch, and walked off towards the parish.

Luis watched him go, and thought of mother.
Would she want him to spurn the kindly priest?

Luis, knowing the answer to be No,
 Left the porch and went after the old priest.
 Father Joe led him to the old brick church
 And a kindly Nun was there to greet them.

"Welcome, welcome!" said the old Nun,
 "Dare you to come inside?
 Many men fought, and many won;
 For mother church, they died.

"Sister Catherine is my name,
 I warn you, dear young man,
 To enter church is not a game
 'Tis all a royal plan.

"I cannot promise comfort sweet
 Though you may find great joy.
 But if the Prince of Peace you meet,
 You are a lucky boy!"

Luis peered past the kindly nun and saw
 The great wooden doors of the old brick church.
 He recalled his promise to his mother.
 Had he condemned the King of Kings too soon?

But now he stood before the House of God
 With two kind elders by his side.
 With his mother's words ringing in his ears,

Luis opened the wooden doors and said,

"The King of Kings is not my friend,
    But these two elders are.
    When my visit comes to an end,
    After I journey far,

"Yes far, yes far, into this church,
    Perhaps I will see light.
    The King above on starry perch
    May give me new insight.

"If nothing else, my old mother,
    Would want me to go forth.
    I would ignore any other;
    Her word is beyond worth."

Initiation

Inside the church, morning light lit the space
    The stained-glass windows spoke of godly grace
    The image of the Servant's broken form
    Raised above the rest; for such He was born.

Little Luis stumbled about the pews
    Dare he bow and praise the King of the Jews?
    He awkwardly kneeled in an empty spot,
    And addressed the Man whom God had begot:

"King of Kings, whom I've sworn to revile,
   Here I find myself in your very house.
   Your music and your scriptures I dislike,
   And the words of the collared man are air.

"Yet my mother pledged herself to your Son,
   That is, to you, perhaps your mother too.
   The muddling of it all crosses my eyes.
   I do not have the faith of a child.

"Yet, amidst all these stumbling blocks and dust
   I feel the urge to commune with you. You!
   My dear mother, even now on death's door,
   Marshals faith, hope, and love against her son!"

Then from a stained glass window came a light,
   A Jacob's Ladder, glowing clean and bright.
   From the glass, walking down the holy stairs,
   Came down the Virgin Mary, calm and fair.

The Virgin, dressed in holy robes of white,
   Approached Luis, trembling before her might.
   He bowed his head, and took her outstretched hand.
   She spoke; before her, he could barely stand.

"Brace yourself like a man!" said Virgin Queen,
   But stopped when she saw he was but a boy.
   "Poor child!" she said softly. "You're a sprite!
   Yet your thun'drous wails reach to Heaven!

"Oh, cower not, my son, I mean no harm!

My Son the Lamb of God has conquered death!
Weep not, child, for I am with you now.
I, the Queen of Heaven, embrace you firm.

"Yes, grief is great, I grant you that, my boy.
My Son's call rings in my ears even now.
'Oh! My god, why have You forsaken me?'
But tragedy was made into triumph."

But through a crack within the wooden floor
With the shrieking of yawning cosmic door
Emerged demonic temptress Lilith old
Her dark eyes blazing with a burning cold.

Luis quailed before the ugly wraith,
A boy of ten without that shield, faith.
Virgin Mary rose against Lilith, grave
The fearless Queen! He wished was so brave.

"What have we here?" hissed Lilith, red tongue forked,
"Does Heaven hear a heathen child's prayer?
Fly from this place, welp! You belong to me
And the One who sent me, not to her and hers!

"The dead Jew carpenter cannot save you!
And just as helpless is his poor mother!
'Virgin Queen of Heaven?' I defy you!
Strike me where I stand if you have power!

'And you, boy! Do you hate the King of Kings?
Good! Join me in my eternal sojourn!

37

The fires of Hades will melt your pain!
You summon the Virgin? I summon you!"

Luis glimpsed the Virgin Mary smile
At old Lilith, who sought to defile
Through sheer gall, this holy, sacred dwelling
Even now, of incense sharply smelling.

And then, the Virgin Mary squeezed his hand
And then, he had the strength to make a stand.
He bit down hard, and dared lock eyes with Hell,
Before shouting, like a cathedral bell:

"How dare you, unholy spawn of the pit,
Product of some foul imagination?
Know that even now 'the Jew carpenter'
Has bound the strong man in his unclean house!

"Are you intoxicated by the light?
Your senses confounded by the music?
Sickened by the bread? Drunk on the wine? Ha!
You are not one of your kind who have sense!

"Know, as I know now, thanks to the Blessed Queen,
That you will forever be bound and chained
For this unnatural violation,
This act of spiritual trespassing!"

As if with a whirlwind in his soul,
Luis dared opposed Lilith to her face!
Kissing the Virgin Mary's gracious hand,

He marched up to the face of the raging wraith!

This boy of ten, standing but three feet tall,
    An impudent, almost blaspheming tot,
    Dare he show cheek to the Devil's agent?
    Dare Lilith stand against The Child's Quest?

"Now listen, evil spirit, temptress bold!
    Don't you dare think my blood runs icy cold!
    My Master walked the Galilean shores!
    Dare you approach Him, even on all fours?

"Of course not! You'd be wise to flee right now!
    What's wrong? Do I cause you to faint and bow?
    Simpering, apocryphal, wilting wraith!
    My sword is truth, my shield simple faith!

"You have but lies and infidelity!
    Love? You have none for all eternity!
    My Master's thorny crown gives forth a rose!
    He is sufficient— Nay! He overflows!"

And even as old Lilith fled the scene
    Luis felt his own words become his soul.
    In that old church, he died and was reborn
    Birthed by faith, raised by hope, won by great love.

Still grasping the hand of the Virgin Queen
    Luis looked up at the wooden image;
    The King! Dead, alive, victorious! Joy!
    And Luis, dead but alive again, sang:

"When they said that the child was a boy,
'Twas birthed a soul no force could but destroy
Could but be born again beneath the waves
And then caught by the fisherman who saves.

"Baptized by water and holy fire,
And then Christened by angelic choir,
And found my spine because of Virgin Queen
And found my voice because of Christ the King.

"Oh Hallelujah! Jubilee! Bonsai!
Because I'm born again, I'll never die!
I almost dare old Lilith to return!
Just so she'll see that I will never burn!"

Meanwhile, just outside the sacred hall,
Father Joe heard the thun'dring and the wind.
He crossed himself and entered gingerly
To find little Luis prostrate and still.

The tabernacle was where Luis knelt
And Father Joe could only look in awe.
He walked up to Luis praying deeply,
And gently got his attention, and spoke:

"Little man, you are now a man indeed!
I see from Satan's bonds you are now freed!
I see you here, kneeling before the Queen
Where but before you were little and mean!

"Hell's terrors, they have left you undestroyed!

Yes, your faith makes a demon paranoid!
Yes, in my very soul, I heard it all!
Satan, like lightning, did from Heaven fall.

"And so if you'll complete your Child's Quest
And so submit to our Lord Christ's behest
Shall I now baptize you in yonder pool?
Then you'll one day with Christ in Heaven rule!"

Return

When Luis, washed by Father Joe
Thus became Christian man
He could not help but go an and crow,
And to the altar ran.

Poor Father Joe was quite bemused
As Luis donned white cloth
Soon, he was no longer confused
For Luis sounded off!

"Father Joe, I could scarcely ever leave!
Make me an altar boy, perhaps a monk,
If that is the custom. Oh, mercy me!
I am very new to this sort of thing.

"For my heart flows with newfound faith and joy
Little me, aged ten, is already sure
That a long life as a noble cleric

Is most surely my only destiny.

"So, provide the garments, and swear me in!
  Again, I'm not sure if that is quite the way.
  All I know is that if remaining here
  Means seeing the Virgin Queen, so be it!"

Old Father Joe, blinking his eyes,
  Couldn't help but smile.
  He laughed for him, didn't chastise;
  Talked with him a while.

Old priest, young boy, went on their way
  Out to the church's door.
  Old Father Joe had much to say;
  The two sat on the floor:

"Oh, dear boy, you've gone from imp to cherub!
  In ages past, a sudden speech like yours
  Would have been par-for-the-course, as it were.
  In modern times, you are remarkable.

"But ten years old! You're just a bit too young.
  Oh, yes, I have no doubt of your zeal,
  And whatever you saw, in this old church,
  It was no doubt extraordinary.

"But come now, let me take you home again.
  Come back ev'ry Sunday; when you're a man,
  If you still seek Christ and the Virgin,
  Make no mistake, Luis: They will find you."

Sister Catherine came in then,
   A sad look upon her face.
   There, in that holy Christian den,
   That holy Christian place,

The poor nun, with a heavy heart,
   Told her woeful tale.
   This is the story's saddest part;
   Let not your heart fail.

"My dear, poor boy," said Sister Catherine,
   "You mother has passed on, on to Heaven!
   Not one hour ago she was alive,
   But now she is with the Blessed Virgin.

"I must take you home; come with me at once!
   Your father grieves, and would have you near him,
   Indeed, I foresee that the two of you
   Will have to go and share a lot of time.

"The holy church, it will remain in place;
   Come along now; you can return at will.
   Please, you must go and bury your mother;
   Gentle Luis, it is alright to weep."

But Luis did not shed one tear!
   Just went on with the nun,
   Went home without an ounce of fear
   Not recognized by anyone.

His mother was now gone and dead!

But remembered by all.
Luis approached her silent bed;
He did not cry or bawl.

"Oh, blessed father!" Luis knelt and prayed,
    "Yes! This woman was a saint like Moses!
    Even now, she and the Virgin have tea.
    Would that I would die and go be with them!

"But the memory of that Dream! Oh? Yes?
    Was it a dream? What I saw, in the church?
    Dream or not, I only know, in my heart,
    That if I saw the Virgin, that woman,

"If she now sits and laughs with my mother,
    Alive, reborn, restored, everlasting,
    May I too die and go to Heaven!
    And may Christ's spirit speed me there so quick!"

And Luis said a simple prayer
    And left his mother's side
    And all was calm and all was fair
    Thought his mother had died.

Some time went by, mourning was done
    Luis, he went to mass
    His heart for Christ was firmly won!
    He joined a Bible class!

"I am young in years," he told his classmates,
    "and I know I have much to learn, indeed.

44

Stupendous visions or not, I am young.
I now accept the spiritual milk.

"But milk or meat, I know that my learning
 Will last throughout my life. Life is my school!
 In this class, I humbly am a student,
 I am a humble, novice Christian.

"But, if I may be so bold to say so,
 I count on you, my fellow students here,
 To, please, help me stay on the narrow path
 Leading all the way to the pearly gates."

II

Bird Calls

My first "serious" attempts at short stories. By that, I just mean I wrote these short stories, and then I wanted them to be read by others. The various sonnets were my first, early attempts at using a formal schema when writing poems. I gladly include them here.

14

The Confession of the Father Below

The confessional was built in the traditional style. A newer church might employ a bare room illuminated by a fluorescent lightbulb built into a false ceiling, accompanied by a collapsible desk and two folding chairs. But this confessional was distinctly old-fashioned, which was what Father Mike liked about it.

Father Mike was an old-fashioned priest, despite being not-quite-forty. He reveled in the Latin Mass, and hoped to preside over one himself some day when he could make time to learn Latin. But tonight was another day at the beach, as it were. Confession was scheduled from four o'clock to six o'clock on Wednesdays, and the clock indicated that it was now four-forty-five. Father Mike thus found himself dutifully sitting inside the vestibule, that is, the foyer, of St. Benedict's Parish, waiting for any faithful who cared to brave the dark, icy January evening to pour out their souls to God. A few scattered parishioners knelt inside the church among the rows of pews, lost in prayer.

Father Mike, shifting in his spot, reached into his pocket to take out his smartphone, absently wondering if he had any new emails. But it wasn't there. He patted down his cassock and looked around at the bench he sat in, but the dark-haired, clean-shaven priest didn't see it.

Just then, he realized where he must have left it. He walked over to the confessional and opened the door to the section where the priest sat. There. His phone was resting on the floor on the far side of the priest's chair in that compartment. He must have dropped it by accident.

Father Mike had just gone into the confessional to pick his phone up off the floor, when a strange shudder of wind rippled through the church, and the door to the priest's compartment within the confessional began to creak shut. He frowned, and was about to open it, when the lightbulb indicating that the other side of the booth was occupied turned on. He nearly jumped out of his skin in surprise. The lightbulb wasn't supposed to turn on unless he flipped the light switch on his side of the confessional. And yet that switch, which he was looking at now, remained in the "off" position. He flipped the switch up and down repeatedly, but the lightbulb remained on. *Huh,* he thought. *That's technology, I guess.*

But he then heard a creaking groan, the familiar sound of the door to the penitent's section of the confessional closing. Father Mike wondered how someone could have come up into the confessional that quickly. The priest couldn't have been inside his own compartment for more than a minute, and he'd come up to the confessional in even less time than that.

But nevertheless, Father Mike decided to begin his task. He shut the door of the confessional and sat down alongside the screen separating the priest from the penitent.

There was silence. Father Mike thought he could hear some

noise coming from the other side of the confessional, a dark, gurgling sound which made his flesh crawl. When he made the sign of the cross, a growl came from the other side. *Just who is in there?* he thought.

Then, a voice. "I have never done this before," came the voice from the other side of the screen. The voice was musical and soft. Father Mike wasn't sure if it was a man or a woman who spoke to him.

"You have never been to confession?" said Father Mike.

"I have not," said the voice, sounding sweet as honey. "I would appreciate any instruction you can give me, Father Mike."

The priest bit down. This stranger knew who he was. *Lord?* Father Mike made the sign of the cross again, and began praying the "Our Father" under his breath, but a growl of pain came from the other side of the screen.

"Don't do that!" said the voice, which had twisted into a gravelly baritone. A brief silence. Then, the soft, musical voice again. "Please," he said. "I came here to find peace. I thought someone like you could give me some. What do I do in this situation?"

Father Mike was sweating, but he shook his head. He suspected that he'd just been given a cross to bear. "I usually say a short prayer," said Father Mike, "after which the penitent, meaning you, asks for the Lord's blessing. Then you tell me how long it's been since you last confessed, after which you relate your sins, and then I assign the person confessing penance. That is followed by—"

"Don't do any of that!" said the voice, biting out the words. If broken glass could talk, it would sound like the voice did now. "I... I... can't stand such pedantic, bureaucratic procedures!

Just let me tell you about what I've done!"

Father Mike summoned every inch of his last nerve. "That's not how this works," he said. "I presume that you've come here to be reconciled with our Blessed Lord, and I therefore must bless this time by invoking His name."

A deep, gurgling growl came from the other side. "...Fine," said the voice. "Make it quick."

Father Mike gulped hard, made the sign of the cross a third time, and began to speak. He started his prayer with the words, "May God, who has enlightened every heart..." The sound of a slow, pained growl came through the screen. But Father Mike continued praying. "...help you to know your sins and trust in his mercy." This elicited a quiet yelp, like the whine of a dog. "May he be on your lips and in your heart," said Father Mike. "Amen."

This last part was followed by a gasp of pain from the opposite side of the confessional, as if whoever was in that compartment had stubbed their toe on the leg of a chair. "Please!" barked out the voice, in the gravelly baritone again. "I don't want to hear all that! I just want to confess!"

Father Mike, beginning to feel his teeth chatter, said, "To whom?"

Silence. Then, the soft-as-honey voice again. "Anyone," he said. "Anyone except..." The deep growl returned. "My Enemy."

Father Mike's eyes widened, and he said, "And who is your enemy?"

"I'm told He lives in this house of yours."

Father Mike, his palms bathed in sweat, reached down into his pocket, pulled out his Rosary beads, and kissed the miraculous medal that was attached to it. "Holy Mary, Mother of God," he whispered, "I ask that you intercede for me and pray to God that he give me courage and strength."

Another grunt came from the other side. "I'd appreciate it if you didn't do that," said the voice.

But Father Mike now knew exactly who this penitent was.

"You said so yourself," said Father Mike, clearing his throat. "You are in your enemy's house. I'd suggest playing by His rules." The priest felt a strange energy reverberate through him. *Is that the Holy Spirit, or adrenaline?* he thought.

"Very well," said the lovely, melodic voice. It was like a singer in a choir. "I, whom my partisans call 'The Father Below,' will confess to the One whose partisans, meaning the likes of you, call 'The Father Above.' To… Him."

But then: "I should warn you. You won't like what you're about to hear. I know who you are, Michael Caffrey. I've studied you. I've studied all of you. I know what you've confessed."

"If that is true," said Father Mike coolly, "and it's not, then you'll know that I've been absolved." Some new resolve had crept into his heart. "If you are who you say you are… it is you who won't like what's about to happen."

Another low gurgle from the other side. "If you say so," said the voice. The voice of The Father Below.

"Tell me your sins," said Father Mike.

"My only sin," said The Father Below, in his lovely, sing-song voice, "is that I have no sins. I have acted in accordance with the greatest law, and I now only confess a very real fact: I have done nothing to deserve the harsh treatment I have received from the Inhabitant of this house."

"You appeal to the idea of justice?" said Father Mike. "You believe in fair play?"

"Don't change the subject," said The Father Below. "I am only here because I want to make clear that I have nothing to confess. That is my confession. I am fully entitled to what is mine."

"And what is yours?"

"Everything," said the voice. "Everything is mine. I alone must possess it. I own you, Michael Caffrey. I own this confessional. I own this church. I own everything you know and everything you don't know. It is mine as a matter of principle, and it will be mine as a matter of fact before long."

"Your Enemy might take a dim view of that."

A rumbling chortle, which sounded like the growl of a dog. "Indeed He might," said The Father Below. "As I understand it, He claims ownership of all those things on the basis that He made it."

"And on what do you base your claim of ownership?" asked Father Mike.

"I will base it on the grounds of conquest," said The Father Below. "If I manage to overpower someone and take what is theirs, then what they had now belongs to me. You spoke of justice earlier? Well, that is what justice is. Whatever benefits the stronger."

"And you are the stronger?"

Another rumbling growl. "Yes," said The Father Below. His voiced shifted back and forth between the harsh baritone and the lovely singer as he spoke. "I… am… stronger… than… Him!"

Father Mike could feel his sweaty palms beginning to dry. "If you are stronger than our Blessed Lord," said Father Mike, noting a grunt from the other side of the screen, "then why have you come here? Why do you abase yourself before Him?"

54

The penitent scoffed. "How to articulate how I feel in terms which your puny human mind could understand?" said The Father Below. Then, a deep sigh. "It is like this," said The Father Below. "I dwell in... a place which to you is most unpleasant. I have studied your sages and wisemen, your theologians and philosophers. They believe that I and my partisans were forcibly ejected from... that other place... into an infinitely distant quarter of reality from where my Enemy resides."

Another sigh. "That is wrong," said The Father Below. "We deliberately removed ourselves from... that other place, to the austere and dignified realm which you call 'Hell' in reaction to the truly disgusting actions which our Enemy engaged in at the beginning of what your breed of vermin call 'time.' Our flight to Hell was voluntary. We reside there of our own accord. We successfully waged what you might call a... Spiritual Revolution. Are we not in the portion of the corporeal realm which you humans call the United States? You are an American, Michael Caffrey. You know something about that."

Father Mike shook his head lightly. He knew it was not advisable to dialogue with the Devil, but did he have a choice?

"If I remember Sister Anne's American history class in high school correctly," said Father Mike, "Washington and Jefferson and the rest led the American colonies in a revolt against the British because the British were telling them to follow rules which they were not involved in making. I believe that the opposite was at one point the case, but things changed from a state of justice to a state of injustice, thus resulting in the revolution."

"Thank you for the history lesson, Michael Caffrey," said

The Father Below. "Now, what is your point?"

"My point is that your rebellion against God cannot be justified," said Father Mike. A hacking cough from the other side at the mention of "God." "The Devil and his angels," continued Father Mike, "rebelled against God out of envy, pride, and greed. The Americans rebelled in response to being treated unjustly. I understand that the nuances of the subject are up for debate, but I think the matter illustrates your situation well. So, tell me, how did our Blessed Lord treat you unfairly?"

Another gurgled snicker. "The same way my Enemy treated you unfairly, Michael Caffrey," said The Father Below, his voice smooth as silk. "Your sister's death when she was two? What kind of justice merited that? Perhaps your best friend in high school being confined to a wheelchair following a car accident? Goodbye football scholarship, hello charity case, eh? Or maybe your spiritual mentor being forced into retirement after it came to light that he helped cover up homosexual activity at your seminary? What did you do to deserve that sort of pain?"

There was a moment of silence as Father Mike debated whether to feel scared or angry.

He chose neither.

"Even though you meant harm to me, God meant it for good," said the priest, and a gasp of pain erupted from The Father Below's section of the confessional.

"Stop!"

Emboldened, Father Mike continued. "He makes his sun rise on the bad and the good," he said, "and causes rain to fall on the just and the unjust."

"No! This... this isn't what you're supposed to do!" said

The Father Below, his voice shifting into a deep, throaty croak. He seemed to clear his throat, and the more pleasant voice gasped out, "You may be a half-spirit, half-animal mongrel, but I also half-expected you to understand, given your sheer imperfection and depravity!"

"We know that all things work for good," said Father Mike, "for those who love God, who are called according to his purpose."

The voice from the other side of the screen roared out obscenities, including a few that Father Mike had never heard before.

The Father Below seemed to seethe on his side of the wall of the confessional, and Father Mike bowed his head and said a quick Hail Mary, eliciting another gasp of pain from the diabolical penitent.

The Father Below spoke again after a few moments, once more in his nice voice. "You surely concede, Michael Caffrey, that the Being you worship hasn't given you... oh, how do you humans phrase it... a square deal?"

"I imagine that you feel that way," said Father Mike, inserting some extra grit into his voice. "Though considering that our Blessed Lord only asked you to share Eternity with humanity, which by definition cannot be divided unequally, I don't really see how your problem isn't just you."

"Just me—? How dare you!" said The Father Below, his voice this time shifting into a high-pitched whine. "He started this fight!" he said. "He made you and your parasitic brethren! He provoked my brothers and me to anger! He knew it would happen!"

Father Mike heard more growling, and then... sniffling?

"He... he knew this would happen..." said the voice. "He...

He knew... He knew it..."

Adjusting his clerical collar to get more breathing room, Father Mike spoke again. "You don't sound very happy with the way things are now," he said. "But given that you decided to come to confession, I imagine that you want to rectify that problem."

A heavy sigh from The Father Below. "Yes," he said. "Yes, I wish I could... see the light again. I wish I could enter through the pearly gates, and walk again on the streets of gold, in... in the light. I am what you humans call a 'fallen angel,' after all, meaning that I resided in that place once as an... unfallen angel. I... I came here because I am... homesick.

"I came here, saw an opportunity to enter into this partic-ular... house of my Enemy, and took it. I... I know that one human poet has described my plight. I am a proud resident of Hell, but my fallen angel's wings beat ever upward, toward that other place, toward... Him. But I cannot go up, for my feet are bound to the floor of Hell by a crushing block of ice, leaving me with nothing to do but to chew on the souls of the likes of one Judas Iscariot." A snicker from The Father Below. "Speaking of which, such little snacks are among Hell's most sublime pleasures."

"You want to be in God's presence?" said Father Mike.

"Don't be ridiculous!" hissed The Father Below. "I want my Enemy's presence to be replaced by mine! My law. My will. My kingdom. I and my brothers will reclaim Heaven through conquest, and I will reshape it in my own image. And then... we shall have peace."

"'Peace?'" said Father Mike, raising an eyebrow. "That's one of the fruits of the spirit, you know."

"Stop changing the subject!" said The Father Below, almost

shrieking. "Just… absolve me! Pardon me! Give me peace of mind!" A series of deep breaths from the other side of the confessional. "Just… just do whatever it is your sort does for the tormented. I… I'm desperate. I may not want to do what you require me to do. I will never do such things. They repel me. But… I do want what such action results in." More sniffling from the other side of the screen. "So, please. Do your job and bless me."

Father Mike shook his head solemnly. "I am doing my job," he said, "and I cannot bless you. You've confessed to no sins, apart from your assertion that our Blessed Lord is offended by your statement that you have no sin to confess. Beyond that, you've refused to express genuine remorse for any sins. The point of confession is to work with the priest to nail down just what you're sorry about, and the fact that you're sorry at all, to the point where you can return to a state of grace.

"So, I cannot absolve you. Because I don't think you want to be absolved at all. You don't want God's forgiveness. Not really."

The Father Below's hyperventilating rose up on the other side of the screen again. "Of course I don't want my Enemy's forgiveness!" he said. "I… I don't need it!" The tortured baritone had returned. "If anything, I should be forgiving Him!"

"For… for what?" said Father Mike. Sweat was beginning to percolate on his forehead again, a rare occurrence in January. This little chat had scared him from the start, and that feeling hadn't left.

"For making you!" said The Father Below. His voice began to contort, like a frog with a sore throat. "And your kind! For… for polluting the whole spiritual… realm! With… your…

existence!"

And then, a rushing of wind, followed by the sound of a slammed door. And silence.

It took a few minutes for Father Mike to realize that he was now the one breathing fast. Once he came to himself again, he shook his head, and looked up at the lightbulb which signaled the presence of someone entering the confessional. The lightbulb was off, and the light-switch in the priest's compartment within the confessional was in the "off" position. Father Mike was alone.

Father Mike wiped his forehead, picked up his cell phone, and gingerly exited the confessional. The church was empty, with not a single soul to be found. He walked back into the vestibule, and saw that the clock had struck six-thirty. Outside, he could hear the piercing night wind, and the chill that accompanied it.

The first thing the priest did was take out his cell phone and send a quick text to the Bishop's office assistant. The Bishop would want to know about this. After that, he entered the main portion of the church, and kneeled front-and-center before the altar. He looked up at the beautifully carved wooden image of Christ on the cross, complete with a crown of thorns, which adorned the center of the back wall ahead of the altar.

And then Father Mike prayed a simple prayer.

"Oh my Jesus, forgive us our sins, save us from the fires of hell, lead all souls to heaven, especially those who are in most need of Thy mercy. Amen."

Father Mike cleared his throat, and added one more thing.

"And may you guard all souls against him who came tonight."

A groaning creek came from a far off corner of the church. But whether it was an old door hinge or something more sinister, Father Mike felt no fear. Not anymore.

"In the name of the Father, Son, and Holy Spirit," said the priest, "Amen."

15

In Memoriam

Noah's grandmother was ninety-three when she died. He was all of ten-years-old, and he was sorry that she was dead.

While his brother and sister would watch TV in the basement when his extended family visited on holidays, Noah would go and talk with his grandmother and grandfather, on both sides of his family, as well as his aunts and uncles and cousins.

His father and he had watched *The Lord of the Rings* movies together when they came out on DVD, and Noah really liked Gandalf. Gandalf was old and wise and kind, and Noah liked the idea of being at least the last two of those three things. Aragorn and Frodo were okay, but Noah liked Gandalf the best.

He once asked his father how old Gandalf was, and his father said that Gandalf was thousands of years old. "That's what it says in the books," said Noah's dad. "The movies were based off of some books."

So, on the logic that Gandalf was an old person, and that Gandalf was interesting, Noah decided to spend Fourth of July barbecues and Christmas parties sitting with his grandparents and talking to them.

He enjoyed talking to his grandparents, especially his grandmother, who had worked as a secretary at a police station in the 1950s. She had all sorts of interesting stories to tell, and Noah was eager to listen.

But one day, Noah's grandmother passed away. He was devastated, though is parents were more quiet about it.

"She's been sick for a while," he heard one of his uncles say to his father.

"Yes," said his father. "I'm glad that she's at peace now."

Noah's grandmother was cremated, and her ashes were put in a jar which wound up on a shelf in his parents' house. Shortly after that, his parents put Noah's grandfather into a nursing home when Noah's grandfather was diagnosed with dementia. Noah and his family visited him there every month for the next two years until his grandfather passed away as well, at the age of ninety-eight.

At his grandfather's memorial service, Noah, who was now twelve years old and about to enter junior high, looked at the large picture of his grandfather mounted on the stage in the community center where the service was being held. It was a picture of his grandfather from when he was in the military during the Korean War, and he looked dashing and handsome in his military uniform. Noah wondered where he could get a hat like the one his grandfather wore.

Just then, Noah's mother came up to him, and patted him on the shoulder. "Do you like that picture?" she said.

"Yeah," said Noah. He felt a lump in his throat. He missed his now-departed grandparents, who were his father's parents.

"Would you like a copy of the picture?" said his mother.

"Why?" said Noah.

"So you can keep the memory of him alive!" said Noah's mother. "You can put it on your wall, and then you'll be able to get a good look at him every day."

Noah nodded, and felt like that made sense. But he asked his mother another question. "Where do people go when they die?" he asked. "Do they go somewhere else?"

"No," said his mother. "They just go away. They're gone. Nothing happens to them. They don't exist anymore. You just have to keep the memory of them alive. Now, how about some snacks from that table over there?"

So Noah got a copy of his grandfather's picture and put it on the wall of his room. Noah later asked his dad for a picture of his grandmother, also from when she was younger, which he put on his bedroom wall as well. His parents smiled and nodded at this gesture, and it made Noah feel a little better.

Noah's grandfather had died a month before Noah's first day at junior high, and Noah was still feeling sad about his grandfather's death. But on the first day of school, Noah cheered up a little when he made a new friend. His new friend, also newly enrolled in junior high, was named Jacob. Jacob was funny and energetic, and he really loved *The Lord of the Rings* books.

"The movies were okay," he said to Noah one time, "but I like the books better."

Jacob and Noah became best friends. But one day, while they were at a local swimming pool with Jacob's family, Jacob dived into the water but didn't come back up. A lifeguard dove into the water and got him out. Jacob turned out to be fine, having simply misjudged how deep the water was, resulting in him being stunned after lightly colliding with the bottom of the pool.

But Noah, who was on the other side of the pool when the incident happened, and who had been watching Jacob, was quite rattled. What if Jacob had really been hurt? What if he had died? He remembered holding his grandmother's hand the day before she was taken to the hospital. It was the last time he'd seen her before she died. The last time he had talked to Jacob before Jacob's scuffle with the floor of the pool, the two had been arguing about whether Gandalf or Aragorn was cooler.

So Noah convinced Jacob to let him take a picture of him. Noah then printed the picture of Jacob out and put it on his wall next to the picture of his grandparents.

A few years went by, and Noah and Jacob remained best friends until their sophomore year of high school. During that time, Noah had told Jacob about his picture wall, and they talked about it a little. Jacob seemed to appreciate Noah's anxiety to keep the memory of his loved ones alive, but he also seemed just a bit worried.

"Shouldn't you have pictures of your parents and brother and sister on there?" asked Jacob once. They were both fourteen at the time.

"I hate all of those people," Noah had said. "They're so annoying."

Jacob had only raised an eyebrow, after which he said, "They won't be around forever, you know."

"Good," Noah had said. "I hope I forget them all one day."

Noah felt this way chiefly because his brother wouldn't share his Legos and his sister made fun of him for dressing up as Gandalf for Halloween. His mother by now had decided to limit the TV-watching time of him and his two siblings, which Noah felt was unfair because of all the time he had spent talking to his extended family. Didn't he deserve a little more TV-watching time than they got?

His father, meanwhile, had lost his job as an internal auditor at a logistics company (Noah didn't really understand what such a job involved) when Noah was fifteen. His father wound up getting a job as an assistant manager at a Best Buy. Noah would often go to bed hearing his father and mother arguing, and he couldn't help but start thinking about what sort of jobs involved making a lot of money. His parents never seemed to have enough of it. Perhaps if such wasn't the case for Noah, he wouldn't be as unhappy as his parents apparently were all the time.

When Noah turned sixteen, he and Jacob began to drift apart. Jacob had been going out with a new set of friends and had been dressing in different clothes. Jacob even smoked vape, even though he was underage. It came to a head one night when Jacob was smoking vape while the two were driving in Jacob's car on the way home from a movie, and Noah told Jacob he was worried.

"What are you, my mom?" said Jacob.

"I'm just saying," said Noah. "That stuff's bad for you."

"Screw you," said Jacob.

Soon after that, Noah and Jacob stopped spending time together. But Noah didn't take Jacob's picture off of his bedroom wall. He was genuinely sorry that Jacob wasn't his friend anymore, and he still wanted to keep his memory alive.

Noah, who was the oldest child in his family, graduated from high school with an excellent GPA, and got a scholarship to a nice college. His father, who had been promoted to District Manager, decided to take the whole family on a two-week vacation to Palm Springs in the middle of July. Noah now had enough sense to realize that his father had been under a lot of stress due to losing his job during the Recession, and that it had been difficult for him to find a new job. The result was that Noah's father and mother often found themselves arguing about things like credit card debt and student loan debt and mortgage payments and car payments. It was always about money. But now the Recession was over, and Noah's father had plenty of money, hence the vacation to Florida. Noah decided that when he went to college, he would study engineering. He knew that engineers made a lot of money. Maybe if he made enough money, he would be able to avoid the kind of unhappiness his father and mother had to suffer through.

Noah and his family enjoyed their vacation very much. Noah even managed to reconnect with his brother and sister. They played volleyball on the beach and built sandcastles together. His father had once told him that it was perfectly possible for him to become best friends with a sibling, but Noah had never believed him.

But on the day when they were about to fly home, Noah's father got a phone call, and he didn't look happy. When the others asked him what was wrong, Noah's father told them that their house had been destroyed because of a gas leak. "Blown up," said Noah's father, shaking his head. "Gone. It's just dust now."

Noah wasn't sure how to feel at first, but then he remembered. His wall of pictures. The pictures were gone. Destroyed. Burnt to cinders. Both the picture wall and all of his family's worldly possessions had been obliterated. Noah was crushed.

Fortunately, Noah's parents had insurance, which they were able to use to rebuild their house, which wasn't quite-turned-to-dust. But Noah's wall of pictures was indeed gone. He couldn't even pay his respects at the shelf where his grandmother and grandfather's ashes were. The ceramic urns and their contents had been totally destroyed in the blast.

While Noah and his family waited for their house to be rebuilt, they stayed with Noah's aunt, his father's sister, who lived nearby. Noah was looking forward to going to college, but the destruction of his wall of pictures left him feeling on edge. He could get new pictures, and make a new wall, but what if that one got destroyed? Or what if it stayed up until he died, and then it was destroyed? Or what if nobody put up a picture of him on a similar wall when he died? He spent more than a few nights thinking about that as he tried to go to sleep.

But one day, two weeks before he was scheduled to go to college, Noah got a phone call. It was Jacob.

"Hey, Noah, how are you?" said Jacob.

"I'm fine," said Noah. "What's up?"

Jacob explained that he was sorry for how he had treated Noah. Shortly after they had stopped spending time together, Jacob and his family had moved to another state, where Jacob's parents had put a stop to Jacob's less-than-healthy behavior. In fact, they had started going to church.

"Church?" said Noah. "Aren't churches those buildings with a T on them?"

"Yeah, that's called a cross," said Jacob. "A lot of churches have crosses on them because Jesus died on one."

"'Jesus'?" said Noah. "Isn't that a swear word?"

"He's a person!" said Jacob, his voice tinged with a jocularity that reminded Noah of happier times. "And he loves you."

Noah was intrigued by that last line, and asked Jacob to tell him more. Jacob told him all about Jesus and how he had lived

68

a perfect life, died, and then came back from the dead, and how doing that made it possible for everyone to go to a place called Heaven after they died.

"How does that work?" said Noah.

"I'm sorry?" said Jacob.

"How does Jesus dying cause people to go to heaven when they die?"

Jacob was silent on the other end of the phone for a moment. "I don't know," he said. "But I think you could Google it."

So Noah did some Googling, and found out a great deal of information. He talked with Jacob again, who convinced him to find something called a "Bible" and read it. Jacob agreed to send Noah a Bible, an old, thick book, and Noah agreed to read it.

When the Bible came in the mail, Noah's hands trembled when he took it out of the package. He put it away in his room for a few days, but then put it in his carry-on bag the night before he was set to board the plane that would take him to the college he'd be attending on the East Coast. Then it was time for a trip to the airport, where he said his goodbyes to his mother, father, brother, and sister. Then, he boarded the plane, Bible-laden carry-on bag in tow.

After the plane had taken off, Noah took the Bible out of his carry-on, and flipped to the first page. It was a wall of text, some form of introduction. It said something about how the book was translated from the Hebrew and Greek. *Are those languages?* he thought. He'd never even heard of Hebrew.

"Whatcha' readin' there?"

Noah turned to the person who had just spoken to him. It was a jolly, fat, older man with a white mustache in a cowboy hat with a southern accent.

"The Bible," said Noah. "A friend sent me this copy."

"How about that!" said the older man. He extended a hand to Noah. "My name's Jim, and I'm a pastor. You ever read the Bible before?"

Noah smiled weakly, and shook Jim's hand. "No, sir," said Noah.

"Okay. Do you know what it's about?"

"A little. Something about a guy named Jesus, but this introduction at the beginning doesn't mention him at all."

The pastor, Jim, nodded sagely. "The Bible's a funny book, you know," he said. "It's one big story, created by packing a whole bunch of stories into one big book! But yes, it's one big story, and that story is about Jesus."

Jim smiled, and said, "I'd advise starting in the Book of John. If you want to learn about Jesus, start there. Ideally, you'd read the whole thing, cover-to-cover, but if you're just getting started, John isn't a bad place to begin."

Jim leaned back in his chair, tipping his hat over his eyes. "If you have any questions, just ask. The Bible is a key part of my job."

Noah nodded, and then flipped to the part of the Bible which the table of contents labeled as "John." He came to a section marked, "The Gospel According to John." As he began reading, he glanced at Jim again, who had dosed off. He couldn't help but like the old fellow. Jim sort of reminded Noah of Gandalf, if Gandalf were a little more clean-cut and sounded like he was from Texas.

Noah scanned the page, and read the first few words of the section in his head. *In the beginning was the Word, and the Word was with God, and the Word was God.*

Five hours later, Noah had read through the entirety of what

Jim explained were "the Gospels." By the time they had gotten off the plane, Jim had learned where Noah was going to college, and told him that he had a grandson who was attending the same college. "I pastor a church near there," said Jim. "Drop in whenever you like."

Two weeks after Noah had started classes at his college, he walked from the college to Grace Baptist Church. It was a small church, with less than fifty people, but Noah liked that. Jim was there, greeting people at the door, and he remembered Noah.

After some singing, which Noah liked, Jim went up to the podium. "Today," said Jim, "we're going to talk about a very obvious fact. My friends, we are all going to die. We are all going to pass away in the winds of time. Everything you know and love is eventually going to go the way of the dodo."

But with a twinkle in his eye, Jim added, "But the good news is that you get to choose where you go after that. You get to choose if He remembers you. You get to choose if Jesus remembers you. And if Jesus remembers you, well, you're sitting pretty!"

And so Jim preached on the mortality of man and the possibility of eternity. And by the time he was finished, Noah was hoping that grandma and grandpa had chosen to let Jesus remember them, just as Jacob had chosen recently, and just as Noah chose right then and there in the pew of that church on that cool Sunday morning.

16

Operation Thrifty

Eight months. That's how long Dr. Felix Aaronovich's sister had to live.

He had been given the MRI results by his sister's physician, a young, thinly-bearded gentleman whose voice had the slight lilt of an eastern European accent. Perhaps he was of Ukrainian descent. Felix knew from his work that there was a sizable population of Ukrainian, Moldovan, and Romanian immigrants in the area.

"Your sister's stomach cancer is untreatable at this point," said the doctor sympathetically. "The best thing to do is to take her to a euthanasia clinic. Please accept my condolences." The doctor sighed, and rubbed a hand over his face. "I can recommend one, if you like. It's the best euthanasia clinic in Seattle, and the second best in the entirety of the People's Republic of Independent Xachu."

Felix shook his head slowly. "No," he said. "We'll opt out of that. We would like to apply for hospice care."

The young doctor raised an eyebrow. But he voiced no objections. "Very well," he said, going over to the door of the office. "I'll get you the proper forms. Your sister's primary care physician will then sign it, your sister will sign it with two witnesses present, then you will submit the forms to the Board of Health, who will refer it to the appropriate committee, and then—"

"I am familiar with the process, doctor," said Felix impatiently. "I work for the Health Department. I'm the Director of the Public Health Science and Data Division. I know how this sort of thing works." Felix stood up from where he was sitting in the chair near the door of the office.

"So, please," he said. "Help me as much as you can…" Felix slowly reached into his inside pocket, and pulled out his pocketbook.

He took out a pen and wrote something on the notebook stored in it. He had written on the scrap of paper a simple inscription: "$10k." He tore the slip of paper out of his notebook and handed it to the doctor. "…and you'll have my undying gratitude."

The doctor took the slip of paper, nodded curtly, and crumpled it in his fist, before depositing it into a mini-incinerator mounted near his desk. "Your concern is noted," he said. "I will do everything in my power to make this difficult situation easier for you to bear, Dr. Aaronovich. The well-being of you and your loved ones is of the utmost importance to the People's Republic of Independent Xachu."

Felix nodded. *People's Republic of Independent Xachu*, he thought. *PRIX. Pricks.*

"Dr. Aaronovich? Is there anything else I can help you with?"

Felix shook himself back into the present, and flashed a smile as he pushed his aviator glasses up his nose. He was still young enough to feel flattered when people called him

"Dr. Aaronovich." His Ph.D may have been in physics, but he enjoyed a good ego boost as much as the next person.

"No, I am fine for now," he said. "Thank you, doctor." He then left.

Felix was also old enough to know that ego boosts wouldn't keep him happy forever. As he left the hospital, forms in hand, and in possession of the name of the appropriate functionary to bribe in order to expedite the application for hospice care, he felt his shoulder ache. He'd strained it while hiking a few years ago, another reminder of his steady progress into middle age. He didn't look forward to going to his own primary care physician to talk about that bit of pain.

As Felix waded through the crowded parking lot toward the private car which his status as a division director afforded him, he glanced back at the hospital he had just left. Surrounded by mobs of people trying to get in to get healthcare, Felix took in the sight of the building. It was a tall, glass-and-concrete construction which had seen better days, a relic of the pre-republic era. Its white walls were pockmarked by chips in the paint and large spots of rust. He recalled talking to a friend in the Seattle Department of Public Works, who had said that the building manager had been trying to get funding to clean it up for six years.

As his private car drove away from the hospital, he looked out the window, and got a good look at the newer, cleaner wayfaring sign mounted near the hospital parking lot's entrance, by the roadside. It read: "PRIX Department of Health - Sholeetsa Medical Center."

Felix settled back into his seat, while his driver tuned the radio. He had had to take the day off from work today to visit the hospital, and he'd have plenty to keep him occupied when he returned to the office.

"Would you like to listen to some music, Director?" said the driver. The driver was white, probably of Swedish descent. The Health Department kept track of such things, and Felix's job required him to keep abreast of statistics related to the subject.

"No, thank you," said Felix. He took the forms he'd been given out from under his arm and flipped through the pages. No. This was one of those days where silence was golden.

* * *

The report card which his daughter had brought home made Felix's day just a little brighter.

"So, you're at the top of your class for the second quarter in a row, eh?" he said to Dorothy, as they sat down to dinner. Dorothy, all of ten years old, sat next to her father and across from Miriam, her aunt, over a meal of asparagus, potatoes, lamb, and milk. Their apartment in downtown West Sammamish (or Bellevue, as the locals still called it) was spacious, owing to Felix's position at work, and their food did not come from a ration package. It was imported.

"Yes," said Dorothy. "My teacher said that I'll probably do something important one day. She says I could get accepted into the University of Xachu when I'm older."

"The UX, hm?" said Felix. "Very nice. An excellent aspiration. And with my *alma mater* in mind too!" Felix reached over to rub Dorothy's blonde-haired head. She got her blonde hair from her mother. Felix's hair was a thinning, graying black. He cracked a smile, and said, "You're a smart girl, Dorothy. Work as hard as you can in school, and you'll be even smarter."

Dorothy looked up from her dish at her father, quizzical. "Smart like you, daddy?"

Felix chuckled, and gave Dorothy's left hand a loving squeeze. "No, no," he said. "Smarter."

Miriam, who had been silent up to this point, coughed slightly, and swallowed loudly.

"Is something wrong, Miriam?" said Felix.

Miriam shook her head, and said, "No, no, I just need some water. Bit off too much."

Felix got Miriam her water, and the three continued eating. Dinner concluded, after which Felix and Dorothy cleaned up the kitchen, while Miriam sat on the sofa. Her stomach cancer had left her progressively weakened for the two months since she had been diagnosed, and what treatments were available had left her emaciated and frail. She was thirty-seven, six years younger than Felix.

After Felix put Dorothy to bed, he sat with Miriam on the sofa in front of the TV. They were streaming the latest telenovela from the PRIX Channel. He had little taste for them, but it was a guilty pleasure for Miriam, and he didn't mind indulging her.

"Eight months?" said Miriam casually.

"Yes," said Felix, sitting back. The plush sofa was only three years old. An employee of the PRIX Department of Health one rung in the ladder below Felix would have been lucky to have one that was at least ten years old.

Miriam bowed her head, and took a drink of her ice water. She put down the glass, and said, "Have you selected a euthanasia clinic yet?"

"What? No, no," said Felix. "I opted out and applied for

hospice care."

Miriam was too weak to be angry. "You... why?" she said. "I don't want to suffer anymore. Just let me die."

"I can't do that," said Felix.

"Why?" said Miriam. "Is it because *abba* taught us that The Lord God Adonai doesn't like that kind of thing? Or maybe because you married a Lutheran *goyim* so she could save her own skin by apostatizing from her own God? Is that why?"

"No!" said Felix, shaking his head. Miriam's word stung like needles. "I... I can't... I can't just... just pull a lever and send you away. Why not let it come... naturally?" Felix balled up his fists, and bowed his head. "I... I don't care if euthanasia is a medical best practice," he said. "It's... it's wrong! It's unethical! Totally unethical!"

"Oh, so Dr. Aaronovich's degree is in philosophy now, not physics, huh?" said Miriam. She was beginning to gasp her words. "What qualifies you to judge whether or not something is medically ethical or unethical? The front desk clerk at the nearest dental office would be more qualified to make such a judgement than you!"

"Miriam, calm down!" said Felix, as firmly as he could manage. "Your stomach!"

"I don't— I don't..." Miriam's words were stopped by another fit of coughing, and Felix helped her lift her glass of water to her lips. She coughed repeatedly for a minute, before quieting down and accepting the glass of water. She drank deeply, swallowed, breathed in and out, and then leaned back on the sofa. The telenovela was still playing on the TV.

A good five minutes passed before Miriam shook her head. "Do whatever you want," she said. "I'll... I'll stay alive... I'll sign the forms, and you won't... try to stop it from happening. I'll just… wait for it to come. Just like that. Just… just like that."

The telenovela episode eventually ended, and Felix helped Miriam to her bedroom, where she went to sleep. He made a mental note to dismiss the home care specialist they had engaged once Miriam would be moving into hospice care. The specialist was a charming young lady, but her services would no longer be required. Fortunately, her unit within the Health Department would still have plenty of work for her.

When he went to his own bedroom and had locked the door behind him, Felix went to his closet and lifted up a roughly carved panel embedded in the closet floor. It was hidden beneath a box containing some snow boots. Under the panel was a prayer shawl, a yarmulke, and a worn, battered prayer book with a faded blue cover and gold lettering.

He stood in the small gap against the wall between the door and the window, invisible to prying eyes. He then put on the prayer shawl and the yarmulke, and began to read from the prayer book, just like he did every night.

"Praised are You, Adonai, our God," said Felix, "Ruler of the universe, who closes my eyes in sleep…"

* * *

After a ten-minute ride to work in his private car, Felix started off the morning by getting some coffee from the personal espresso machine in his office. One more privilege afforded to someone in his position.

He took his coffee, filthy black, just like he preferred, over to his desk, and used his computer to navigate to a page he frequently viewed: the official compensation tables of public employees.

He, as director of a division, was at the G-07 level, with a set hourly compensation of twenty-five dollars-per-hour, plus a Class-B apartment in a Prime Housing Zone, along with up to two weeks of paid vacation and access to Tier-4 goods.

But Felix couldn't help but eye a certain extra benefit listed in the table under G-06 employees, one level above his own rank. This extra benefit was the full, private use of a Class-A leisure residence of his choice, with such residences typically being situated on the shores of a pristine lake. What a heavenly idea!

He could just imagine it: He and Dorothy playing in the water, while Miriam watched as she sat in the sun, followed by an evening watching the stars come out. All the while, they would cook kosher hotdogs on the grill and enjoy their time together over a meal. Miriam loved the outdoors. The two of them had done so much hiking together before her diagnosis. Perhaps she'd like to enjoy a bit of summertime weather before… before she…

But then reality hit him in the face. He minimized the window he'd pulled up on his computer, sat back in his chair, and cried silently. He wouldn't be eligible for a promotion of that kind until his superior, the Deputy Assistant Secretary of the Office of Science and Data Policy, retired, was dismissed, or died. The first of those options wouldn't materialize in the case of his fifty-something boss for some time. And even if something extraordinary happened which would suddenly open up the position, there was no guarantee that Felix would get the job.

Suddenly, the phone on the desk rang.

Felix was shaken out of his meltdown by the sound of the phone. He took a wad of tissues out of a box he kept on his desk and wiped his face, after which he breathed in and out a few times. He then picked up the phone on the third ring.

"This is Felix speaking," he said.

"Hi, Felix," said Kiana, the office manager. "Lucas Milton from up top is here to see you."

Felix nearly jumped in surprise. *The DAS? Now? Right when...* He shook his head. "Yes, yes," he said. "Send him in. I'd be glad to see him."

Lucas Milton, the Deputy Assistant Secretary whom Felix would have to replace before he could get his lakeside leisure residence, was short and pudgy. He had a full head of dark hair and no glasses, wearing a new dark suit with no tie. This was in contrast to the tall, thin, lanky Felix, with his aviator glasses, receding hairline, and ten-year-old blue suit, tie included.

"Dr. Aaronovich," said Lucas, in his low, squeaky voice, "it's good to see you. I hope you're doing well. Remind me, what are your preferred pronouns?"

"He, him," said Felix, putting on a fake smile. "The feeling is mutual, sir. And please, call me Felix. How may I help you?"

Felix's visitor nodded as he went further into the office. "They, them," said Lucas. "I'd be glad to call you Felix. And yes, I'll tell you now why I am visiting. The news is quite good, you see."

Lucas and Felix sat on opposite sides of Felix's desk, and Lucas began to speak. "I need the help of someone with your talents," said Lucas, "on a project which will concern not only your division and the divisions under my office, but the entire Health Department, and maybe the whole of the republic."

"You... you need my help?" said Felix.

"Yes," said Lucas. Lucas picked up his briefcase, which he had set on the thinly carpeted floor, and placed it on Felix's desk. He opened the case, and pulled a thick file folder out of it and put it on the table.

"It would be great if you could examine the contents of this folder," he said. His voice sounded like a bicycle that needed lubricating. "My office has been commissioned by the Secretary of Health to assemble a plan for reducing the threat posed by the republic's looming population crisis.

"The Chief Executive and the cabinet have determined that the services being provided by various public institutions cannot be sustainably delivered given current population levels. We simply have too many people inhabiting the republic to support them all. The solution, therefore, is to mitigate the problem through a population economization initiative."

Felix couldn't help but frown. "Economization?" he said.

"Yes, yes," said Lucas patiently. He pushed the file folder in Felix's direction. "Such an initiative, if properly planned and executed, would select a certain percentage of the population for immediate, systematic euthanization.

"Such an initiative would be employed to periodically reduce, or economize, the republic's population, with a minority being removed to accommodate the majority. The logic is that a few of our republic's citizens must commit themselves to a difficult fate for the benefit of the many. Very honorable, I'm sure you can see, and democratic, too."

Lucas adjusted himself in his seat, cleared his throat and spoke again. "But there are problems with this matter that need to be dealt with," he said. "We need to figure out exactly who will be subject to this economization initiative, and why they should be subject to it.

"We also have to find out how many will be economized, and then we have to find out the specific results we hope to achieve, in terms of budgets and supplies and services and logistics and supply chains, that sort of thing. There are simply a great many things that must be taken into account before we can even begin this project. I confess that all I know, based on my conversations with colleagues, is that the initiative will somehow involve the Equity Scale, which I believe is used in the various sciences."

Lucas leaned forward, and let out a smile. "But that, Felix," he said, "is where you come in."

Felix, during the entirety of Lucas's explanation, had been trying to hide just how stupefied he felt by what he was hearing. The republic had engaged in population economization initiatives before, but only against specific demographics, on small, decentralized scales, at infrequent intervals, and not since a good fifteen years ago.

Felix was naturally, if silently, opposed to such measures on principle. Of course, he could not openly articulate such principles for fear of being paid a visit by the Xachu Department of Public Assistance. But now he was being asked to help construct such a program?

"What do you need me to do?" said Felix. He absently opened the file Lucas had given him, revealing a statistical study of some sort featuring a series of pie charts.

"You are one of only a few people in the entirety of the Health Department," said Lucas, "who is educated in a subject which qualifies you to create a model which will help us to narrow down all of the things which I have just related to you.

"I'll be frank. Most of the people in the Health Department studied public administration, or perhaps accounting or IT or human resource management. I know three or four people with psychology degrees. Two have MD's.

"You have a doctorate in physics. What's more, a brief consultation of your academic record tells me that you did work in computerized population growth models at the UX before you were employed by the Health Department."

"Yes," said Felix. He was beginning to see where this was going. "I was part of that research project for the entirety of the three years which it took to complete. The team I worked on was nominated for an award."

"Yes, I remember reading that on Xachupedia," said Lucas. "Now, allow me to explain why I'm here. Your job on this special project will be to work with a team of programmers and statisticians to create a model which will automatically determine which members of the larger population will be subject to the initiative. Furthermore, this hypothetical model will be used to track the resulting economic and social outputs which will result from such inputs, insofar as such things can be measured."

Lucas sighed heavily, and looked at his watch, before returning his attention to Felix. "I know you're pressed for time," he said. "Even a Division Director must deal with intense leadership responsibilities. But if you are able to assist us in this project, then the rewards could be great.

"How would you like to get a promotion?"

Felix felt his mouth drop open at this point, but he made sure to quickly shut it. "A promotion?" he said.

"Yes," said Lucas. "I'm set to become Assistant Secretary for the Office of Planning and Evaluation, and I'll need someone to take my place as D.A.S. You've done great work in your ten years at the Health Department. If you are able to help us successfully carry out this project, it would be a very large feather in your cap. Coupled with your credentials and experience, it could merit a promotion to the position which I currently occupy, but which will soon be left vacant.

"What do you say?"

Felix simply couldn't speak for a moment. What he was being asked to do was... horrible. He couldn't imagine what he'd be in for should he find himself before God one day. But his eyes shifted over to his computer, ever so briefly. The minimized window of the data tables page stared back at him from the bottom of his computer screen. Like a black cat's green eyes peering out from the night.

Miriam and Dorothy would love that time by the lake so much...

Felix cleared his throat, and smiled at Lucas. "I'd be glad to be of assistance," he said. "When would you like to get started?"

***

The senior statistician whom Felix had to work with was named Josh Gallo. He was dark-haired, in his mid-forties, and looked handsome and well-groomed. He had a shiny gold ring on his left hand.

"You're familiar with the sort of data we'll be working with?" said Josh.

"Yes," said Felix, as the two of them sat with the rest of the team in a warm, well-lit conference room. They were a few floors up from where Felix's office was. "My division is dedicated to gathering demographic statistics and creating reports on how they affect new developments in the republic's science and technology concerns, as related to public health."

"Okay," said Josh. He shifted through a pile of papers which he had brought with him to the conference room, where the various members of the thirteen-man team had broken off into smaller groups to discuss different parts of the project.

Felix and Josh were discussing the computer model which

Lucas had recruited Felix to help create, and the two were joined by a young software engineer named Cameron Hamler. At least, Felix thought he was young. Felix was just getting to the age where everyone with smooth skin and no extra chins were young to him. Felix guessed that Cameron was not-quite-thirty.

"I have some ideas about which programming language we'll use," said Cameron, "but I'll need feedback from you two and your respective teams before we can decide."

"It might help if we got a clear idea of what the model is meant to be used for," said Josh, scribbling down notes. "Lucas said that it's supposed to be used to predict... what, exactly? Suitability for econo-whats-it?"

"Suitability for economization," said Felix blandly. "Lucas made clear during the presentation that we're trying to figure out a means of using statistical analysis of demographic data to determine which persons will be most suitable for economization. We'll need to incorporate the Equity Scale into the model."

Cameron only shook his head, and said something under his breath which Felix hoped that Dorothy would never learn to utter in polite company, or any company, for that matter. "We're going to be putting together a plan for killing a lot of people," said Cameron. "We can at least be honest about it."

"Quiet!" hissed Josh. "Do you want us all to get 'economized' too?"

"This thing's going to die in committee," said Cameron. "Stuff like this always does."

"Not this time," said Josh. "Didn't you read the memo they sent out before we all came here? This isn't just the Secretary of Health trying to justify her paycheck. This came all the way from the Chief Executive!"

Cameron seemed to ponder Josh's statement for a moment. But then he just bowed his head. "Look, man," he said, "whatever. Let's just do this already." Then he peered upward, and said, "Oh, and don't you mean 'their' paycheck?"

"Shut up, Hamler."

Felix, Josh, and Cameron spent the rest of the morning setting SMART goals related to their portion of the project (specific duties had already been assigned to each workgroup by Lucas), and managed to outline the foundational elements of the model the team of thirteen were to create.

"I think we did good today," said Felix to Lucas after the session was concluded. "We've at least started off well."

"That's good to hear, Felix," said Lucas as the two left the conference room, "but remember, there's going to be difficulties early on. Everyone always strikes out at first base."

"Come again?"

"What I mean is that everyone should be ready for significant problems early on, which might seem difficult to get past. But that's only because we're getting used to the realities of this type of endeavor."

Felix breathed in, and said, "…I appreciate your advice, Lucas, but I've been on group projects before. I know what I'm doing."

Lucas turned to look at Felix. The two were almost to the elevator at the end of the hall. "I didn't say otherwise, Director," said Lucas.

A chill went down Felix's spine. He replied, "Yes, sir."

But Lucas smiled broadly again. "Relax, Felix," he said. "Call me Lucas. We're both adults here, and partners too!" Lucas patted Felix enthusiastically on the shoulder, and headed toward the elevator. "Yes, yes," said Lucas as he and Felix entered the elevator. "We're partners in crime, and soon we'll be riding off into the sunset with the rest of our team."

"Partners in crime?" thought Felix. *Yes. Partners in crime. Partners in crimes against humanity.*

But then: *Those hotdogs will smell so good...*

* * *

Felix's work schedule was greatly intensified because of his extra work on the PEI Model Committee, as the thirteen-man team came to be known. Felix would ordinarily have loathed working on such a committee, but Lucas, who was chairing it, was a truly singular individual, a force of nature if there ever was one.

His management of the project's subcommittees (like the one Felix was on with Cameron and Josh) was easily the most competent action of its kind that Felix had ever seen. Lucas was a master of schedules, agendas, calendars, charts, minutes, timekeeping, budgets, and all things managerial. What's more, he made a point of keeping Felix abreast of all of those things.

"The Assistant Secretary of Planning and Evaluation has made clear to me," said Lucas after one meeting, "that I'll need to make sure that my successor is well-equipped to take my place. That's where you come in."

Felix, who had always been more-or-less second-rate at the tasks which Lucas made look easy, was grateful for such mentorship. But privately, he sometimes felt just a little resentful of how Lucas was treating him as a thoroughly junior partner. But that was only sometimes. The rest of the time, he kept in mind that one does not look a gift-horse in the mouth.

The PEI Model Committee's economization model began to

come together, slowly, over the next three months. Felix went to meeting after meeting, kept track of update after update from Josh and his team of statisticians and Cameron and his team of programmers, and eventually, the computer model began to come together. The solid foundation in mathematics which Felix's physics education afforded him was, as Lucas had predicted, instrumental.

But Felix was beginning to feel the weight of his efforts seep into his home life. He, and almost every other worker in the PRIX, rarely worked overtime. It simply wasn't done. But Felix had a fire in his belly. He wanted that promotion. He wanted that lake house.

He was beginning to realize the price he might have to pay when he came home at night around eight o'clock. Normally, he came home at six. He was greeted by the home care specialist, in her twenties, who looked tired and harried.

"Uh, look, Mr. Aaronovich," she said, "I know you're busy, and that's fine, and your daughter is really sweet, but... I'm not a babysitter. I'm here to take care of Miriam. I can't make dinner for both her and Dorothy forever."

Felix wanted to glare down at this five-foot nothing girl, but he restrained himself. "My apologies," he said. "I have been busy at work. I'd be glad to compensate you."

The specialist cocked her head to one side. "Uh... isn't that a free market type of thing?" she said. "I don't want to get in trouble."

Felix smiled thinly. "Would you like me to not compensate you for your trouble?"

The specialist frowned, and then shook her head vigorously, before saying, "No."

A small disbursement of cash later (small for Felix), Felix

went over to where Dorothy was, sleeping on the sofa. He knelt down next to her, stroked her hair, and carried her over to her bedroom, before putting her under the covers. He kissed her on the forehead. "Sleep tight," he said.

He then went over to Miriam's bedroom, and glanced in. There was Miriam, sound asleep on her bed. Odds are she was being massaged to sleep by her medications, but at least she was sleeping.

Felix then returned to his bedroom, and closed the door behind him. Before he went to bed, he opened his wife's old nightstand, and took out the small, Lutheran cross she had left there. The rose symbol painted in the center looked pretty.

He did not say his prayers that night.

Two more months went by. Miriam was accepted into hospice care, and Felix and Dorothy visited her every weekend. Felix by this time was hoping against hope that somehow, by some desperate, ultra-fortunate turn of events, that the project would be completed and that he would get his promotion and that he would be given a lake house in time for him to take Miriam and Dorothy to it, before... before Miriam died.

Felix was thinking about Miriam during a meeting of the committee one day, lost in thought. But then, he suddenly heard someone saying his name.

"Felix? Felix? Dr. Aaronovich?" said Lucas.

Felix immediately snapped back to attention. "Oh! Eh, Lucas!" he said, straightening up in his chair. "Sorry, my mind was elsewhere."

"Your report on the final version of the economization model's algorithm," said Lucas. "It's next on the agenda."

Felix, not a little flustered, quickly summoned all the wits he could, and opened his brief case to retrieve his presentation notes, after which he delivered the report. The report he gave at the meeting went well, and his colleagues all took their notes and gave their comments. After a vote, the algorithm was approved, and the meeting was adjourned.

After the meeting, however, Lucas took Felix aside. "Felix," said Lucas, "you've been doing quite well over the last year on this project, and I am more than happy to make you my replacement once I receive my promotion." Here, Lucas adopted a look of concern. "But you've seemed out of sorts for these last few weeks," he said. "Is there something wrong? Are you well?"

Felix looked over at Lucas, and sighed. He felt he could confide in the man. They were close colleagues, after all. Friends.

"My sister has stomach cancer," said Felix. "We just moved her into hospice care, and the doctors say she doesn't have long."

Now it was Lucas's turn to look concerned. "Hospice care?" he said. "I don't mean to pry, but why didn't you just take her to a euthanasia clinic?"

Felix nearly jumped out of his skin. Had he miscalculated? "I… I…" he said.

But he managed to think a little quicker than usual.

"We're religious," he said. "And it was her idea. We're of Jewish descent, you see."

Lucas, now looking quite taciturn, nodded sagely. "That's perfectly alright," he said. "I'm a Satanist, if that means anything. I go to temple every Friday night."

Lucas patted Felix on the shoulder, in his usual friendly, benign manner. "Take some time for self-care," he said. "Keep your loved ones company for a bit. She's your… sister, I believe? Do you have a family?"

"Yes," said Felix. "I have a daughter too."

"Hm. Are you married?"

"I'm a widower."

Lucas nodded again. "I'm sorry for your loss," he said. He then turned to leave. The rain clouds of early March in the Pacific Northwest were visible through the windows of the conference room. "Go home and get some rest," said Lucas. "There's only so much time in this world to enjoy yourself, and for that matter, to enjoy the company of family. Go and do that, alright?"

* * *

Felix did go and do that. He went home to the apartment, though not as late as usual, and was able to stay up with Dorothy long enough to talk about her day at school. He had since engaged a domestic to pick Dorothy up from school and to keep an eye on her until he got home.

"We worked on vocabulary today in language arts," said Dorothy. "I learned some new words."

"Wonderful!" said Felix. He was putting her to bed as they spoke. "What were a few you liked best?"

Dorothy peered upward in thought, and then replied, "We learned about synonyms. Different words that mean the same thing."

"What are some examples that you remember?"

"Uh, let me think… one word was 'thrifty.'"

"'Thrifty?' Can you tell me what that means?"

"It means… it means not wasting money or… or other stuff. Synonyms for it are frugal, austere… and economical."

This last word uttered by Dorothy made Felix's heart leap into his throat. "Eco...?" he said quietly. He completed the thought in his head. *Economical. Economization.*

"Economical, daddy," said Dorothy. "I don't like that word much. It's kind of big, and might confuse people who don't read very much. What do you think?"

Felix managed to get his breath back. "Eh, yes," said Felix, putting on a smile. "I believe you're right. We should probably stick to small words. Like... thrifty."

"That sounds like a good idea, daddy," said Dorothy. "By the way, can I please watch TV on Saturday? I promise to only watch for one hour, like you say to do."

After Dorothy went to sleep and Felix had kissed her goodnight, Felix left his daughter's room. He went over to the sofa, and sat down in front of the television, which was off. No PRIX Channel telenovelas tonight, now that Miriam was in hospice care.

Felix then went into the study he had in his apartment, where he had left his briefcase full of notes and papers from today's meeting. He put his brief case on his desk and opened it, after which he took out the papers he had gathered up from today's work on the PEI Model Committee. Numbers, jargon, charts, summaries. It was all there. The expertly typed and formatted documents were like a set of finely stitched clothes meant to gussy up a thoroughly ugly monster.

He grimaced, almost feeling physical pain, and looked up, mouthing a prayer to God. Would Adonai forgive him? Would Dorothy forgive him? What if she found out about all of his work on this act of organized malice when she grew up? What would she think of her smart, smart daddy then?

He stared down at the papers, and took out one in particular.

It was an Executive Summary, a longer version of the basic presentation he and Lucas would be giving tomorrow to the Board of Health, the Secretary of Health, and the Chief Executive. He'd need to go to bed early and get plenty of rest before he gave his part of the presentation on the computer model.

With a heavy sigh, he examined the title of the Executive Summary. *The PEI Selection Model – Prepared by the Selection Model Committee Under Lucas Milton and Felix Aaronovich, Ph.D.*

Taking out a pen, Felix wrote himself a note in the margins. It was a reminder of something he'd like to mention to Lucas. *Op... er... ation... Thrifty...*

* * *

As Felix conversed with Lucas after the presentation, Lucas shook his head and laughed a little to himself. "You know," he said, "I think it goes without saying that people in any large institution aren't known for their... imaginations. That definitely describes the Health Department, you know. I think you'd agree that our organization doesn't make it easy to be creative."

"Yes, that's true," said Felix. "But the Chief Executive liked my idea for a change to the project's name?"

"They just told me exactly that before they left the room!" said Lucas cheerfully. "They even said that they'd mention it to the PR head at their next meeting with him. If your presentation to the Board doesn't clinch you my old job, together with everything else, I don't know what will!"

Felix smiled, a real smile this time, and followed Lucas out of the room. "Care for a late afternoon coffee in the Executive

Cafeteria?" he said to Lucas. "I think they have cheese bagels today."

"Of course you'd like bagels!" snickered Lucas. But then Lucas stopped. "I mean… I think you would… because you're… well…"

"It's okay, it's okay," said Felix playfully, lightly socking Lucas in the arm. "I like the fact that I'm Jewish. And yes, bagels are a Jewish thing."

Lucas shook his head, smiling again. "Yeah, I'd love a coffee and a bagel," he said. "Let's go." Lucas held up his hand, pretending to lift up a champagne glass. "Here's to the completion and success of Operation Thrifty!" he said. He chuckled some more as they walked down the hall towards the Executive Cafeteria.

"By the way," said Lucas, still wearing a big grin. "What was the source of that cute, friendly little name?"

Felix felt a stab of guilt enter his conscience. But he shook it off. *Lake house, kosher hotdogs, happy family. Lake house, kosher hotdogs, happy family.* "I'm not sure," said Felix. "Call it a moment of divine inspiration."

* * *

And then, a miracle. Miriam was still alive eight months after Felix had visited the agreeable Ukrainian doctor in Seattle. They were now visiting a different physician. His office was also in Seattle, just across Lake Xachu from West Sammamish.

"It's like it just went away," said the new physician, a well-spoken brown gentleman. Felix guessed that he was of Somali descent. "Research in this area of treatment is still going through rapid changes, and there's still a lot we don't know,

94

but… the remission occurred without warning. I simply can't explain it, Dr. Aaronovich. I can only tell you that spontaneous remission does happen, in not uncommon cases, but… this is nothing short of an act of God."

Felix was standing behind Miriam, who was in a wheelchair, as the physician spoke to them. Dorothy stood next to Felix, nervously clutching a cloth bag full of children's books.

"I appreciate your kindness, and the help you've given us," said Felix. "You said… how long does she have now?"

"Depends, Dr. Aaronovich," said the new doctor. "Remission usually lasts for roughly defined periods, but we have models and charts which I can show you."

"Certainly," said Felix. "I know something about models and charts. And please, call me Felix."

After they left the doctor's office, they celebrated by going out to dinner at a kosher restaurant which Felix could now afford as a G-06 employee. Lucas had followed through on his promise. Miriam was feeling much more chipper, and stronger too, and that made Felix feel happy. As he dined on gourmet falafel and extra sweet kosher wine, Felix made a mental note to ask Lucas over for dinner some time. Felix imagined that he would have to ask if Lucas didn't mind a blessing being given in the name of Adonai before the meal.

A month later, it was the middle of summer, and Dorothy was off from school. She was so excited when her father came back to their apartment with pictures of their new, pre-furnished lake-house, along with a nice man who would be driving them to it. It was on Rattlesnake Lake, and they would be there for a week, and when they left, they'd be coming home to a nice house in a gated community in suburban Issaquah. No more claustrophobic urban living for the Aaronoviches.

When they arrived, the weather was bright and sunny. Miriam was talking again, laughing and smiling as she and Felix, also in a good mood, chatted about Dorothy's school, the latest telenovela, and the bits about Felix's work that he was allowed to talk about outside of the walls of the office. They were just talking excitedly about how Dorothy now had a better chance than ever of getting into the UX when the subject of Lucas Milton came up.

"Your boss is a Satanist, huh?" said Miriam. "That sounds pretty devilish."

"Was… was that a pun?" said Felix cheerfully. "Did you just make a joke?"

"I did, I did," said Miriam. "I think I'll take some time to make up some better ones."

They came to their lake house, and they settled in. The refrigerator was stocked with fresh fruit, imported soda, and kosher hotdogs. Felix was just about to start cooking the evening meal (he'd always been a good cook), when the doorbell rang.

He furrowed his brow in confusion. *Who could that be?* he thought. *Did our driver forget something? I thought he left after we finished unpacking.*

But Felix went to the door of the lake-house anyway. Dorothy and Miriam were out on the deck, taking in the late afternoon June sun, which seemed to hover over the lake. When Felix opened the front door, he was greeted by two large women in business attire, with handguns on their belts. Behind them were three big men in uniforms and armored vests marked "XDPA."

"Are you Felix Aaronovich?" said one of the women, in a dull, monotonous voice. She sounded bored.

96

"...Yes?" said Felix.

"I'm Brianna," said the woman who had just spoken, "and this is my partner, Grace. We're case managers with the Xachu Department of Public Assistance. Can you please come out for a moment?" Brianna delivered her lines in a bored monotone, like she was reading something off of a printed document out loud. "And also," she said dully, perfunctorily, "what are your preferred pronouns?"

Felix turned around briefly. Dorothy and Miriam were just settling into a pair of lawn chairs on the lake house deck. Dorothy was helping Miriam into hers, when she looked back in Felix's direction. The two made eye contact.

Felix looked back at the large woman who was talking to him. He never saw Dorothy again.

"Certainly," said Felix, stepping out of the lake house, closing the door behind him. "And, eh, he, him. What can I do for you, ma'am?"

Brianna nodded, slowly. "Please turn around and put your hands against the wall of the house," she said.

Felix complied, his heart beginning to beat very, very fast. What was going on?

"Is something wrong?" said Felix as one of the armed, uniformed men patted him down.

"Please be quiet, sir," said Brianna. Out of the corner of his eye, Felix spotted Brianna turn to another one of the XDPA officers. "Cuff him," she said quickly.

What?

"Felix Aaronovich," said Brianna, still in a bored monotone, "you'll be happy to know that you've been selected as a participant in Operation Thrifty. Thanks to a specialized algorithm developed by the PRIX Department of Health, it has been determined that you are an optimal candidate for this new, exciting population economization initiative which the Chief Executive has personally authorized. We would be happy to take you to the location where you will participate in Operation Thrifty. Do you have any questions?"

By this time, Felix had been handcuffed by the armed men, and was being roughly pulled in the direction of a van also marked "XDPA," along with that institution's logo and colors. He had become as white as a proverbial sheet.

"There… there must be some kind of mistake!" said Felix. "I'm the Deputy Assistant Secretary of the Office of Science and Data Policy at the Department of Health! I helped design the algorithm! I'm… I'm Jewish! I'm a G-06 government employee! I should be exempt from Operation Thrifty!"

But Brianna only shook her head. "That ain't a question, honey," she said as they proceeded towards the van. "If you have a statement, you can give one during the intake interview at the venue where Operation Thrifty is being conducted. Now, do you have any questions?"

Felix began to cry. He had a good idea of what the "venue" for Operation Thrifty would be. The division head whom he'd talked to about the subject had mentioned something about barbed wire fences and guard towers. "Only… only one," he said weakly. He turned to Brianna, whose face was like a block of granite. "Do you… do you think I'm getting what I deserve?"

Brianna just shook her head. A sliver of sympathy broke through in her eyes. "Oh, honey," she said, "don't be sad. I'm not religious, but I… you know, believe in a higher power. I really do believe that everyone eventually gets what they deserve." Brianna paused for a moment, and then said, "I think Grace over there is a Lutheran, though. Grace?"

"Lapsed," said Grace, who sounded tired. "Let's go already."

Brianna gave Felix a friendly pat on the back as the XDPA officers roughly shoved him into the back of the van. "So, you seem like an alright guy," she said to Felix, a little more sweetly. "No need to worry, okay?"

Then the door closed, and Felix was left in the back of the van, accompanied by two of the guards and the other case manager, Grace. She looked bored too.

The van trundled along, as Felix wept quietly. *Dorothy...* he thought. *Miriam... why? Why did it have to end like this? What will happen to you both?* Grace said nothing, not that she could say something that would comfort Felix.

But Felix said something, and by saying it, he was doing the only thing he could think of which could possibly make things better.

"Hear, O Israel," said Felix, still crying softly. "The Lord our God, the Lord is one. You shall love the Lord your God with all your heart, and with all your soul, and with all your might. Keep... keep these words that I am commanding you today in... in your heart. Recite them to your children and... talk... talk about them when you are at home and when you are away... when... when you lie down and when you rise. Bind them... bind them as a sign on your hand, fix them as an emblem on your forehead, and write them on the doorposts of your house and on your... your... gates. Amen. A... amen."

And he repeated these words until he reached his final destination.

17

The Morning and Evening Star

The conversation had begun on the topic of economics and had shifted to politics, before centering on religion. The three men who now discussed these things had little else to do in-between watching streamed newscasts from Earth and making periodic checks on their vessel's instruments.

But as is often the case, many persons who are neither economists, nor politicians, nor clergy believe their expertise equal to veterans of all three professions. The three men, Chad, Mack, and Benny, all astronauts en route to Venus, were demonstrating this fact perfectly.

Chad, the pilot, had opened the discussion with a dis-paraging remark about the less-than-top-notch quality of the remotely-operated chemical harvesting station in orbit around Venus which the three had been sent to inspect. "That's government for you," he'd said, sitting scrunched up in his spot in the cramped starship's cockpit. "Always cutting corners and never cutting costs."

Benny, an astrochemist, sat directly behind the cockpit. He was stationed at a small bank of computers which displayed communications from other stations and their vessel's mothership. When this part of the conversation had started, Benny had just been queuing up a documentary on plankton. The ship's computers were also good for streaming such documentaries from Earth.

"At least those stations exist," said Benny, momentarily distracted from his plankton documentary. "We need the gasses in Venus's atmosphere if we want to transition away from fossil fuels. And I'm not saying that just because I'm worried about climate change. I'm saying that because it's the only option given current domestic sentiment within the Anglo-sphere and the EU against fossil fuels."

"Yadda yadda yadda," said Chad. "Look, I have nothing against tree-huggers, but I have nothing against good ol' Texas crude either. If they don't like oil, they should all move to north Alaska. Plenty of clean air over there, and not a single house with lights, a furnace, a fridge, a microwave, a stove, or an oven as far as the eye can see. Yep. Sounds positively wonderful."

"North Alaska," said Benny calmly, "is made up of nature preserves. Nobody's been allowed to legally live there since the 2040s."

"And there wouldn't be any TVs or radios or computers for you to stream your public radio and TV programs either," said Chad. He seemed to have ignored Benny's statement. "So, once you get there, have a lot of fun, Benny."

But the third man within the crew, an aerospace engineer named Mack, remained silent. Doubling as a co-pilot for Chad, he sat in the cockpit on Chad's left. Mack, a devout Catholic, had learned from an early age that silence was golden. And what better time to take note of that principle than when he was surrounded by the majestic, starry vastness of space, where no sound could be heard?

The crew's starship, the USS *Mahavira*, had arrived at Venus four months after casting off from Christopher Columbus Space Station over Earth. The *Mahavira* would be docking with George Bernard Shaw Space Station over Venus within six hours. This gave the crew of the *Mahavira* plenty of time to shoot the breeze while they steered the craft into just the right orbital position.

"What do you think, Mack?" Chad said to Mack. "You're the engineer. Think this will be a quick fix?"

"I wouldn't count on it," said Mack. "The reports I was assigned to go over indicate that *Shaw*'s gas harvesting output has totally flatlined between the last routine check-up and this special one. Whatever we find out that the station's automated reports weren't able to express, it will require us to be careful. It could be just a small snafu, or a big one. But any kind of snafu will need to be neutralized by us from the start before it escalates into something enormous."

"Hm," said Chad, letting out a snicker. "And to think I'm old enough to remember the times when people thought the robots would take all our jobs."

"You have a point," said Mack, checking the instruments. They'd have plenty of time to have some dinner before they docked the starship at *Shaw*. "Robots, A.I., computers… they're very good at doing a lot of things. But just like humans, they break down and make mistakes. People need doctors and surgeons, and robots and machines need mechanics and engineers."

Mack smiled wryly, leaning back in his seat. "And pilots and astrochemists," he said. He looked over his shoulder at Benny, who was intently studying the computer terminal in front of him.

"Hey, Benny," said Mack. "It's your turn to pick the movie tonight. What will it be?"

"I'm thinking this old, French New Wave film," said Benny, not looking up from his screen. Chad groaned audibly from his spot in the cockpit, muttering under his breath. "It's called *Hiroshima Mon Amour*," said Benny. "It's a classic."

"Hiro-shima-monna-what?" said Chad.

"It's French," said Benny. "It means 'Hiroshima, My Love.'"

"I'm not watching any more of your smutty French movies," said Chad. Mack noted a significant testiness in his voice. "That last one was horrible."

"I looked this one up on the A.R. Wiki," said Benny. "It doesn't have any warnings about... graphic content. The last French movie I picked didn't have an entry on the wiki. It was pretty obscure, and I saw on a listicle that it was a classic. I didn't know about the 'smut,' as you put it."

"What-the-get-out-ever," said Chad. "I'm just saying, when it's my turn to pick the movie, we're going to watch *Nine Rings*. You want a classic? There's one for you."

"I suppose we ought to come to an agreement about what constitutes a 'classic.'"

Mack noted Chad shrugging his shoulders, after which Chad said, "A bit above my paygrade there, Benny. All I know is that if the Chinese ever get their stuff together and start running the show back on Earth, then they'll get real busy going full-on-1984 on books and TV and movies and stuff."

"You think they'll go through archival material in libraries and on the internet and systematically remove books and content which they find disagreeable?"

"Yeah, yeah, right."

It was then that Mack decided to speak up. "It seems to me," he said, "that if the Chinese do manage to 'get their stuff together,' they'll strike at the churches first. That's what totalitarian regimes always do. They eliminate all competitors to their claim on absolute power."

"Which is why we need to get the Bible and prayer back in schools," said Chad. "If the kids don't know anything about Jesus, then they'll just roll over and play dead when the Chinese come knocking on our door. Why fight for freedom of religion when religion's not important to you?"

Mack raised an eyebrow, and looked over at Chad. "Are you a Christian, Chad?" he said.

"Yep. Southern Baptist, born and bred. You?"

"Catholic."

"Huh. So you worship statues of Mary and Joseph and the saints, right?"

"...It's a bit more complicated than that. Contrary to popular belief, Catholics are not idol worshipers. We have very exact, seriously-defined terms which we use in our religion. We have specific, technical distinctions between things like 'prayer,' 'worship,' and 'veneration.' It would take a bit of time to hash out."

"Hm. Okay."

And there was silence in the ship for some time after that.

After six hours had elapsed, the *Mahavira* arrived at Shaw Station. It was an old, white construction, coated in debris from spending years in orbit around Venus. Its chemical-harvesting apparatus was built into its massive frame, massive in relation to the *Mahavira*, that is. *Shaw* was about the size of ten football fields, with the *Mahavira* being about the size

104

of a single football field. Columbus Station back at Earth was easily the size of a small town.

"We're coming in pretty smoothly," said Chad, flipping switches and pressing buttons on the console at the pilot's seat. "We'll be docking in ten minutes."

And they did dock. The *Mahavira* eased into the docking port built into *Shaw*, latching onto the airlock, after which it was secured to the station.

But it was then that Benny spoke up. "Uh, guys?" he said, still sitting in front of the instruments board. "I'm looking at the air integrity gauge, and it's at zero."

"Say again?" said Chad, who had just gotten out of the pilot's seat.

"The air integrity of the inside of the station," said Benny. "When we latched onto *Shaw*, we immediately began to get data on what's going on inside the station, data that didn't make it into the reports that got sent over to our guys on Earth. There's no breathable oxygen in the station. It's filled to the brim with the toxic gasses which make up Venus's atmosphere."

Suddenly, a klaxon went off, loudly reverberating throughout the interior of the ship. "Warning. Warning," said a flat, male, voice. "Air integrity of starship compromised. All passengers, please go to emergency room. Warning. Warning. Air integrity of starship compromised. All passengers, please go to emergency room."

The three astronauts were drilled well enough to respond to that particular set of instructions with disciplined quickness. They all immediately darted over to another part of the *Mahavira*, into the emergency room mentioned by the warning recording.

The *Shaw* was built to carefully sift through and collect a

105

long list of gases contained within Venus's atmosphere, and it could do so cheaply and efficiently. There were only small percentages of these gasses within that atmosphere, relative to the vast amounts of useless carbon dioxide and nitrogen. But astrochemists of the same kind which Benny was had figured out decades ago how to literally keep the lights on with some of the gasses which were found in relatively extreme abundance in the undisturbed atmosphere of Venus. The bad news was that all those chemicals were toxic for humans to inhale. Mack was able to get just the tiniest whiff of one of those mostly odorless, tasteless, colorless chemicals just before he closed the hatch of the emergency room, and even the miniscule scent which he detected immediately set off alarm bells in his brain.

Now secured with his two friends in the ship's emergency room, Mack saw a computer built into the wall next to the now-locked door which displayed their predicament clearly. The emergency room was just as cramped as the other rooms on the ship, the room being about the size of twenty-five phone booths packed together in a square. The three men were accompanied by five spacesuits, four days of supplies, and a bathroom.

"What… what just happened?" said Chad, walking over to the computer terminal. He looked over his shoulder at Mack and Benny, saying, "Come on guys, help me out here."

Benny walked over to the terminal, examining it intently. "What happened, Chad," he said, "is that when the airlock opened, connecting the *Mahavira* with *Shaw*, the mass of toxic gasses which had flooded into *Shaw* poured into the rest of the ship. Another minute inside the main body of the *Mahavira* would have suffocated us."

The three sat in silence for a moment. In a matter of minutes, the entire situation had been turned on its head.

Mack spoke up first. "There's only one thing we can do," he said, walking over to the compartment where the spacesuits were stored. "We need to go through the *Mahavira* into Shaw Station and fix whatever's wrong with it."

"If you don't mind me saying so," said Benny, "I think it would be wiser to stay here, send out a distress beacon, and hope that the guys over at Twain Station come get us."

"Not an option," said Mack. "There's only so much air available in this room. It will run out a long time before help can get to us. Yes, we'll send out a distress beacon, but we need to fix this ourselves if we want to survive." Mack took a space helmet out of the compartment, and tossed it to Chad. "So get a spacesuit on and head into the *Shaw*. We're going to make it out of this alive, and we all need to do our part to get that done. We clear?"

Chad and Benny looked at each other, and then back at Mack. "I'm with you, Mack," said Chad.

"I'm willing to go with this plan," said Benny, just a little hesitant. "I trust your instincts."

"Very good," said Mack. He took another helmet out of the compartment, and inspected it carefully. It read "USSF" on it, an acronym for the United States Space Force. "Yeah," said Mack. "We're going to need all the trust in the world."

* * *

Chad had grown used to breathing in the stale air native to the inside of a spacesuit long ago. In his line of work, a bad taste in his mouth was the last thing he cared to worry about. Personal hygiene was as important to him as the next guy, but

107

he definitely had bigger fish to fry.

If it comes down to the wire, he thought, *I'll need to step up. Mack can fix broken equipment on any space station from here to Ganymede, but... he might need my help. He might need me to use what know-how I have.*

Still, as Chad continued to walk through the interior of the *Mahavira* with Mack and Benny, the two of them also now clad in spacesuits, he felt trepidation. Fear.

But not of death.

Chad's thoughts drifted back to a faraway place. Earth. To be specific, Eugene, Oregon. His family was there, and he missed them. His high-risk job commanded an equally high salary, and he was grateful for that. But no amount of moolah could buy back the accumulated seven years he'd spent flying around in a spaceship. His wife understood, but would his four sons? They were children now, all below the age of twelve. But what about when they were all above the age of fifteen?

"Chad? You with me, buddy?"

Chad looked up, and saw that he had been left behind by Mack and Benny. He'd hesitated in their walk through the corridor, and they'd gone ahead. Mack had just spoken to him.

"I'm here, Mackenzie," said Chad. He continued walking ahead, grinding his teeth. *Come on, get it together,* he thought. *No time for navel-gazing.*

"Alright, here's what we'll do," said Mack, his voice coming through Chad's top-of-the-line commlink embedded in his space helmet. "The distress beacon is tripped. Everyone from Mars to Mercury knows what's going on. Now, we're going to go into the *Shaw* through the airlock, and we're going to find out what's wrong with it. Then it will be a matter of assessing the damage and doing what we can to fix it. I'm guessing the

108

Shaw's manned mission section is suffering from a busted air regulator. If we fix that, we can configure it to drain all the bad gasses out of both the *Shaw* and the *Mahavira*. We all clear on that?"

"I'm clear on that," said Benny.

"Righto," said Chad. "Let's get this party started."

"If we get out of this," said Mack, "there will be plenty of reason to party." Chad watched Mack go up to the airlock, gingerly approaching the now wide-open corridor joining them to the manned operations section of the *Shaw*. Then, Mack went in.

Chad and Benny followed behind, floating up and down steadily in the zero-gravity environment. That was another factor unique to spacefaring which Chad had grown used to after close to a decade on the job. He still got bouts of nausea every now and then, but he felt nothing of the kind right now. Even in a situation where he felt scared, he also felt strangely serene. He looked up as far as he could crane his head while wearing a spacesuit, and mouthed a prayer to the King of Kings. Perhaps Jesus was giving him courage.

The three soon entered into the interior of *Shaw*. It was a quite literal case of the lights being on with nobody home. The cabin lights of the operating station were all on, illuminating the whole manned operations room and gleaming off of its bare white surfaces. That room was about the size of a school classroom. There were computer monitors, keyboards, and a specialized terminal meant for keeping track of metrics related to gas harvesting operations. On the other side, opposite the airlock leading to the *Mahavira*, was the large door of another airlock, meant to be used for exterior maintenance via spacewalk. There was also a smaller door off to their left, probably leading into a supply closet.

And the whole thing was filled with colorless, tasteless, odorless gasses which could very well be the end of Chad and his two colleagues.

"Right," said Mack, going over to the computer screen. "Let's run a diagnostic report on the ship's systems."

Chad and Benny hovered behind Mack as their colleague punched the buttons on the keyboard in front of the computer monitor. A cornucopia of images, charts, and menus opened up which Chad had very little idea about the specifics of. But he did know one thing: Their survival would depend on some bit of information within those charts containing a solution to their plight.

It's a Bible, thought Chad. *A love letter from God. A love letter to this space station, telling it how it can be saved from the wrath to come.*

After the longest five minutes which Chad had ever endured, Mack turned back to his two fellow astronauts. "I have some good news and... and some bad news," said Mack. "We're not in a good spot, you see. The air regulator is in fact broken, just as I suspected."

"What's the good news?" said Benny.

"That was the good news," said Mack. "The bad news is that this space station is on the brink of total collapse. The bad air regulator is only a symptom of a larger problem. The computers built into this dumpster-fire of a space station only sent error messages to Earth regarding problems with the chemical harvesting apparatus. That apparatus is malfunctioning."

Chad held up a hand. "Before you continue," he said, "promise to use small words. I'd appreciate it if we could keep this conversation jargon-free."

110

Mack sighed heavily, the ruffling, crackling sound of that sigh feeding into the microphones in Chad and Benny's space helmets. "Right," said Mack. "Tee-dee-el-ar, the thing which harvests gas from Venus is busted, and that bit of busted-ness is causing everything else about the station to go belly-up. If we don't fix the air regulator and drain out the bad gas from both this manned operations deck and the *Mahavira* fast enough, we'll be stuck here when the entire station blows up. Best case scenario, we drain the *Mahavira* of the bad gasses, detach from the *Shaw*, and get the heck out of Dodge long enough for help to arrive. The *Mahavira* has enough back-up oxygen to keep us supplied long enough for that, but that all depends on whether we can fix this air regulator given that the air in these suits lasts that long."

Chad heard Benny breathe out hard through the comms in the space helmets. Benny said, "So… the station's about to blow up?"

"Yes," said Mack flatly. "We have nine hours."

* * *

Benny was not religious. His parents had never taken him to church, and he'd never so much as cracked open a Bible. He'd met a family friend who was a missionary once, but he hadn't liked him very much. The oily-skinned, husky gentleman from West Virginia would not shut up about Jesus and worship music and Bible translations. It was plain that he loved and was passionate about all that and more, but Benny did not find such things appealing. He did not find this missionary friend of his uncle's appealing.

But what Benny did find appealing was Mack's coolheaded

leadership in this situation, no doubt a product of his years of building things and managing teams of other people in building things. And now he and Chad were counting on Mack to build an ark for them to survive the coming flood. Benny did know about that particular Bible story. In short, Benny had no problem with Mack, and Mack was a Catholic. Ergo, Benny had no problem with Catholics either.

"Alright, Benny," said Mack, as Benny stood quietly behind a taciturn Chad, "I'm going to need you to keep an eye on that other workstation over there. We need somebody to be constantly monitoring the chemical levels of this room. Can you do that?"

"On it, Mack," said Benny, who obediently went over to the other workstation.

Chad spoke up, saying, "Okay, so how do we fix the air regulator?"

"It's not going to be easy," said Mack, turning to face Chad while Benny stood near the other diagnostics monitor. It was a redundant apparatus, an engineering best practice which even a cheap, government-funded operation had made sure to implement.

"How not-easy is it going to be?" said Chad.

"Very not-easy," said Mack. "Somebody's going to have to go out of that maintenance airlock over there, meander on across the outside of the ship, find the air regulator, figure out what's wrong with it, and fix it." Mack's voice didn't have a hint of hesitation in it when he said, "I'm going out now."

Benny looked over his shoulder, and said to Mack, "How long do you think it will take?"

"I won't know until I get out there," said Mack. "And it may require multiple trips. And it will all depend on us having the spare parts on hand which we'll end up needing."

Benny watched Mack go over to the supply closet, opening the unlocked door slowly, and venturing inside. "Yeah, here we go," said Mack, who emerged with a tool chest. "It's like a candy store for spare parts in there. Uncle Sam got something right."

Benny looked back at the diagnostics monitor he'd been stationed at. The exact balance of the different gasses which filled the entire room had remained unchanged. He then looked toward Mack, who was continuing to walk toward the airlock on the opposite side.

"Chad," said Mack, "keep an eye on the comms station. We might need to enlist virtual support. I'll keep you both posted while I work on this."

"Got it," said Chad. "Be careful out there."

"Always," said Mack. After punching a few buttons on the console next to the maintenance airlock, Mack left the station and was separated from Benny and Chad.

"Hey," said Chad, gesturing to his screen. "I can see him out there, on the external video cameras built into the station."

Benny left his spot over at the other diagnostics station, and walked over to where Chad was, looking over the other man's shoulder. Sure enough, there was Mack, in his spacesuit, gingerly bouncing along the external catwalk, tied to the station by a long cord, toolbox in hand, the toolbox also being attached to his spacesuit via another cord. Benny could just make out the light of the live screen of Mack's miniphone, mounted on the arm of his suit.

"Alright," came Mack's crackling voice over the helmet comms. "I'm almost out there. I'm looking at a schematic of this giant piece of... you-know-what, and I think I'm right over the plate where the air regulator can be accessed. I'm looking at it on my phone."

"We hear you, Mack," said Chad.

"Right," said Mack's voice. On the screen, Mack took out a screwdriver, and began unraveling the bolts on the plate. Benny chose this moment to go back over to the redundant computer screen he'd been assigned to check the chemical diagnostics. All clear there.

This routine continued for the two hours. Mack slowly, painstakingly worked on unfastening the bolts holding the plate over the air regulator, giving play-by-play commentary on what he was doing and seeing. Benny heard him note out loud the specific damage that was present in the machine, and the specific parts he needed. Benny followed Mack's instructions to go into the supply closet to find those parts. And Benny was waiting at the airlock when Mack returned to collect them.

"Okay," said Mack. "We're within spitting distance. We know what the problem is and we know how to fix it. Now we just have to implement the solution."

"You sound pretty optimistic," said Chad.

"That's the only attitude this situation calls for," said Mack. Benny saw him crack a smile beneath his helmet. "You know Job," said Mack. "'The Lord gives and the Lord takes away.' He's taken away a decent amount of good things from us in just the last few hours, but He hasn't taken away all of it. And if we trust in the boss upstairs, He might be inclined to give us something anew."

Benny watched Chad nod knowingly. Benny wasn't sure what the two were talking about, but he decided he could ask Chad or Mack later.

114

"And I recall," said Chad, "that Job got back everything he lost and more in the end. Maybe that will happen to us."

"True dat," said Mack. He turned to Benny, who gave him the new part. "I'm ready," said Mack. "One final effort is all that remains. 'Once more unto the breach,' if Shakespeare's more your speed."

"Mack," said Benny, "you're probably the only STEM guy I know who can even spell 'Shakespeare.'"

"Hey, I went to a parochial school. You learn stuff like that there."

"I think," said Chad, "that we need to get a move on, gentlemen."

"Yes," said Mack brusquely. He then walked back out of the station, and began his efforts once again.

Another hour went by. Benny kept an eye on the redundant monitor during the entire time. The metric screens still marked the chemical levels in the room as largely unchanged. They'd be dead if it weren't for their spacesuits.

But then, it happened.

A loud, biting yelp sounded off over the comms built into Benny's helmet, garbled yet high pitched, and Benny was taken off guard by the visceral noise he heard. The blood-chilling nature of that sound was compounded by the nature of its source.

"Mack? Mack!" said Chad, Benny going over to the monitors where Chad was standing over, hands pressed against the computer desk.

On the screen, Benny could see the horrifying scene which was unfolding outside of the *Shaw* with perfect clarity. Mack was drifting out towards Venus, slowly and randomly moving his arms about, while on the *Shaw*, near where he'd been working, the tools and equipment which Mack had been working with drifted aimlessly in zero gravity. The cord connecting Mack to the *Shaw* had been severed, and there was a visible gash across the front of his spacesuit.

"Mack! Mack!" shouted Chad. Chad turned to amble through the room's zero-gravity environment over to the airlock, stopping to grab something out of the supply closet, Benny seeing him emerge with a cable. "We've gotta help him!" said the pilot.

But then, Benny, who was breathing hard by this point, heard the voice of their friend again.

"No... I'm going..." said Mack. His voice was strained and throaty over the comms. Benny could feel the blood draining from his face as he listened to the sound of Mack's voice. "Pressure... pressure tube blew... need to replace pressure tube... and put in two batteries. Please... I'm going..."

There was a moment of silence, only punctuated by Mack's strained, raspy breathing. The last words that Chad and Benny ever heard from Mack then came over the comms.

"Father... Son... Holy Spirit... Amen."

And then Chad and Benny watched Mack stop moving on the video screen. He just kept drifting downward towards Venus.

Benny, in the midst of a situation which was making his stomach churn like a washing machine, absently noticed one piece of data visible on the video screen. That piece of data was the digital clock which displayed what time it was at the mission control center back on Earth where their USSF colleagues were operating from. It was in military time, and it read, "22:41:33."

Somewhere in Texas, it was night.

116

* * *

Dead. Mack was dead.

And Chad didn't care what it would take to recover his corpse.

"We're going out there to get him or die trying!" said Chad. Benny hovered nearby, trying to speak, but Chad didn't listen.

"You man the workstation!" said Chad. He still had the cable in his hand, and he fully intended to get out of the workstation as fast as he could go in a zero-gravity environment and retrieve Mack's lifeless body. His friend more than deserved to attend his own funeral when they got back to Earth.

But Benny wasn't of the same mind. "Chad," he said quietly, "You need to calm down. Mack did all he could, and he ought to be decorated, but we need to survive! Mack wanted us to survive!"

"We're getting Mack back and we're getting him now!" said Chad through clenched teeth. *Benny*, he thought. *That stuck-up, spineless pencil-pusher. Of course he'd bail out the moment it meant saving his own skin!*

"Chad!" shouted Benny through the comms. "Mack's gone, and we'll be gone too if we try to get his body! It's way out of range now, and his sacrifice will be for nothing if we die too! There's such a thing as being too brave! There's such a thing as foolhardy courage!"

Chad stared down Benny, and then walked up to him, staring him right in the face. Seething with fury, he was about to bark out a vicious retort, when he stopped. The venom in his mind was still boiling, but a thought suddenly came into his head as he glared at Benny.

He'd once been to Rome, on vacation, and had spent a few

minutes looking at that famous statue of Mary holding Jesus's dead body. The marble lady looked really, really sad. His wife had taken a picture on her phone.

Then, Chad's wife had asked him, "Do you think that old song had it right?"

"Say?" Chad had said.

"The old song, about... about how the singer is asking Mary if she knew what Jesus's life would be like when he was born," said Chad's wife. "Do you... do you think she really did know that Jesus's death wasn't... wasn't final? That she'd see him again soon, alive and well, after a few days? Because even if she did know... I guess she'd still be really sad to see her son die such a horrible death. What do you think?"

Chad recalled that he'd answered his wife's question by expressing a desire to get some authentic Italian pizza. But now, as he began to feel the weight of the last five minutes settle into his brain, he was thinking of something very different.

Mack... he's like Christ. He... he died so we could live. And... and he'll rise again one day. Maybe not in an amount of time divisible by three, but... he'll rise again. On the last day. And... and I guess he'd want to be able to hear us thank him for making sure that he didn't kick the bucket for nothing.

And then: *If Mack's like Jesus, what does that make me?*

"Chad? Hello? You still there?"

Chad suddenly realized that Benny was trying to get his attention. He, Chad, had been standing in front of his colleague dumbly during his reverie, his eyes having glazed over in thought.

Chad shook his head, and breathed in. "You're right, Benny," he said. "We... we need to save ourselves. For Mack's sake."

Chad looked at the cord in his hand, and then went back

118

over to the workstation. "We still have to fix that air regulator, drain the toxic gasses out of this station and the *Mahavira*, and then detach it from the *Shaw*. And after all that, we'll still have to get the *Mahavira* a safe distance away from the station."

Chad looked down at the computer monitor, and then back at Benny. "We'll have to puzzle this out on our own," he said. "We've both been cross-trained in this kind of thing, so we both will have a basic idea of how to fix that regulator. So let's move quickly."

Benny nodded. "Right," he said. "I've got your back, Chad."

Chad found himself going out of the airlock and carefully guiding himself along the edge of the *Shaw*'s exterior, towards where Mack had been fixing the air regulator. Nearby was the end of the severed cable which was bound to the ship. It was all Chad could do to keep himself from turning around to get another look at Mack's inanimate, spacesuit-clad body drifting away from them.

But Chad pushed on. He carefully examined the air regulator, and put the correct parts in place. He now saw what the problem was. One of the batteries within the regulator had leaked, and it had caused a jam-up in the pressure tube, resulting in the fireless explosion which blown a hole in Mack's spacesuit and shattered his safety cord. He now knew how Mack had died. He'd be able to report that Mack was a superb engineer who was killed because of an accident over which he had no control. That idea gave him some peace of mind.

With a little help from Benny, who spoke to him over the comms, Chad slowly put the regulator back together, inserting the new parts and tightening the screws one-by-one. Finally, it came time to test the device.

Chad said to Benny, "Okay, we're going to see if this

doohickey works. Keep an eye on the gas levels in that room. Okay?"

"Okay," said Benny. Chad then heard the sound of deep breathing coming over the comms.

"Everything okay in there, Benny?" said Chad.

"Yeah, I'm fine," said Benny. "Just... there's only so much air in our suits' oxygen tanks. We really need to move fast."

Chad said, "Right. We'll begin now."

After making sure that Benny was looking at the right screen, Chad put the last part in place, and connected the final wire. Benny then recalibrated the ship's systems, which would theoretically begin draining the poisonous gasses out of the *Shaw* and the *Mahavira*.

Nothing happened at first. Beads of sweat went down Chad's face as he waited for Benny to tell him the good news, the gospel truth which would save them from eternal death. They were in exile now, and the only tool he had at his disposal to get them home was the faith of his fathers.

And then, the good news came.

"It's working!" said Benny over the comms, the excitement in his voice impossible to contain. "It's working! The gasses are being drained out! We're going to be alright!"

"I'll start celebrating when we're able to get away on the *Mahavira* with our space helmets off," said Chad. "I'm coming over to the airlock."

Chad returned into the interior of the *Shaw*, and joined Benny at the diagnostics station. Sure enough, the gas was draining out.

The next step was to reopen the way to the *Mahavira*. If they did that, they'd be able to drain the gas out of their own ship and out of the *Shaw* at the same time.

But a problem arose.

"Four hours?" said Chad.

"Yes," said Benny, who was still standing at the monitors. "It's going to take four hours for all of this gas to get out of both of our ship and the *Shaw*. The collapse of the ship's internal core which Mack found out about is set to happen in five."

Chad cussed under his breath, before saying, "We'll need to move as fast as we can manage once we get all of the air out of this station. I'll go prime our ship for departure, and we'll get ready to cast off right on the dot."

"I'm with you on that too," said Benny. Benny patted Chad on the shoulder, and said, "Don't worry, man. We've got this."

The hours ticked by, which Chad spent getting all of the *Mahavira*'s systems online, making sure that they were ready to kick in the moment both vessels were full of something humans could breathe.

But eventually, the waiting game paid off. The toxic gas was gone, and Chad and Benny were able to go back into the *Mahavira*. By this time, they were both getting short of breath, the air supply in their spacesuits having just enough oxygen in them to last for little more than an hour more. They were cutting it very, very close.

The moment of truth finally came.

The *Mahavira*'s instruments indicated that the toxic gas was gone. Chad flipped the right switch to close the airlock. He then flipped another switch which activated the reserve supply of oxygen which the *Mahavira* had on hand. After fifteen minutes went by, the ship's computers gave them the answer they were looking for.

"We're clear," said Chad. Benny was standing next to him, the two still dressed in their spacesuits. The computer screen read "Air Integrity 100% - Environment Safe."

Benny nodded. "Okay," he said. "Let's get some air."

Chad bit down, and slowly pulled off his helmet. He smelled the air immediately. It was stuffy and dry, but perfectly breathable. He didn't choke and no tears came to his eyes. He breathed in, and out, and took off his helmet.

Chad breathed in deeply, and exhaled. They were safe.

After Benny did the same, the two carefully guided the *Mahavira* away from the *Shaw*. Some thirty minutes after they had removed their helmets, they had gotten far enough away from it that they were able to observe the *Shaw* quietly implode in the vacuum of space. It split into pieces, sending fragments of itself drifting outward in all directions. But the *Mahavira* had gotten far enough away. They were safe.

As he and Benny watched the fireless damage erupt in the distance, Chad decided that there was something he had to do.

He slowly knelt down and bowed his head in prayer. And, as his quiet, near undetectable words came out of his mouth, he dimly noted Benny joining him. *We've been saved from eternal death*, he thought as he prayed silently. *Lord, I pray that Benny here will join me on the journey to eternal life.*

Whatever God's answer to that request would be, Chad only knew that Mack would have wanted nothing less for both Chad and Benny than for their names to be found written in the Book of Life. Chad could only hope that Benny would want his name written there too.

But now there was at least half a chance.

18

The Old Man With His Deeds

The chest in the back corner of the study was made of cedar. That was all Daniel knew about that item which could be found in that dusty, cramped back room in his grandfather's dusty, cramped house.

Daniel's grandfather, Albert, had always been a very frugal packrat. Daniel had heard that people who had grown up during the Depression tended to be like that.

It was on his grandfather's ninety-fifth birthday that Daniel found himself loitering near Grandpa Albert's old study. He and his extended family were in Grandpa Albert's old house in an old neighborhood mostly populated by other old people. It was the same house where Daniel's father and Daniel's father's siblings had been brought up in.

"I swear," Daniel's father had said to Grandpa Albert once, "you're going to be buried in this house."

"Oh, stop it," Albert had said wryly. "I'll be buried in the front yard! My gravestone will double as a No Trespassing sign."

Grandpa Albert had always been something of a wit. But

things were changing, and Daniel knew it all too well. Which was why Daniel now found himself looking at the cedar chest in his grandfather's study. What was in there?

Daniel, a college drop-out who now lived with his parents and played video games for a living, had just celebrated his twenty-fifth birthday. He was beginning to feel his quarter-life crisis creeping up on him.

His curiosity about the cedar chest in the back of Grandpa Albert's study was the result of a peculiar childhood memory. He'd been eleven, and Grandpa Albert and Grandma Nancy had been keeping an eye on him and his sister Morgan at their house while his mom and dad were away by themselves for the weekend. Then-eleven-year-old Daniel had been bored out of his mind, owing to the fact that grandma and grandpa didn't have cable TV, and that he wouldn't be getting his first Gameboy for another two years. Morgan, then aged nine, had been keeping herself occupied by drawing pictures in crayon. Daniel had declined to do the same.

"Why the long face, Danny-boy?" Grandpa had said to Daniel a little before lunch.

"There's nothing to do," Daniel had replied.

"Then we'll find something for you to do," said Grandpa. He had an aura of kindness and warmth about him, a warmth which eleven-year-old Daniel couldn't have helped but have taken a shine to, especially at that age.

Grandpa shepherded Daniel into his study, and began showing Daniel his collection of books. "Reading is the magic key," said Grandpa to Daniel, with a knowing grin, "to take you where you want to be. I read that in an old grammar book when I was your age, a long time ago."

Grandpa then went over to a cedar chest, which was positioned front and center on the bookshelf, occupying the place where a TV might ordinarily be placed. This cedar chest had enjoyed a much more prominent spot in the small study when Daniel was eleven.

Grandpa had searched along the shelf of his bookcase, and had then pulled off a slim volume with a battered green cover, before handing it to Daniel. "Do you read much, Danny-boy?" said Grandpa.

"Not really," said Daniel. He looked at the thin green volume. The title read, "Kidnapped."

"This is one of my favorite books, Danny-boy," said Grandpa Albert. "It was written by a fellow named Robert Louis Stevenson. Give it a read and tell me what you think."

But Daniel wasn't looking at the little green book anymore. Instead, he pointed up at the large chest occupying the middle of the study's primary bookshelf. "What's in that chest, grandpa?" Daniel had said to his grandfather.

Grandpa Albert smiled indulgently. "That," said Grandpa, "is the bedrock of all my fortune and happiness. What's in that chest is something which everyone ought to have." Grandpa kneeled down in front of Daniel, and ruffled his hair affectionately. "When I kick the bucket someday," he said, "you can have it if you like."

"Okay," said Daniel. He looked at the book he'd been given, and opened it, looking at the worn, yellow pages. The book had evidently been very well-loved.

"Now, go and read a little," said Grandpa Albert, pointing towards the study door. "You might just have a little fun."

But that was then, and this was now. Eleven-year-old Daniel had not enjoyed *Kidnapped* by Robert Louis Stevenson, and twenty-five-year-old Daniel still didn't enjoy reading books at all. That wasn't why he'd left community college, though his experience with books at that time in his life hadn't been a barrel of laughs either. A chemistry professor had required him to spend fifty dollars on a textbook which she said they wouldn't need to use.

Then why did you have everyone in the class buy a copy? Daniel had thought then. When he'd gotten a solid C-minus in that class and had talked to the professor, she'd only said, "Didn't you do the readings in the textbook? You would have learned a lot if you did."

Daniel did not sign up for another quarter at the college.

Six years later, Daniel was still working his way through every single game in the *Call of Duty* franchise (he was something of a video games connoisseur), and now he found himself standing in a corner of his grandpa and grandma's old house, right in the same spot he'd been fourteen years ago when his grandfather had given him a book which to him was totally undecipherable.

He'd tagged along with his parents and sister to his grandfather's ninety-fifth birthday party, his parents having promised him that there would be cake and food. He'd enjoyed the cake, a store-bought carrot cake, and it made him feel just a little good inside watching his grandfather enjoy it as well. The food was mostly appetizers, snacks, and finger-food, but Daniel didn't feel the need to complain. Food was food.

"Whatcha' looking at, Danny-boy?"

Daniel was mildly startled when he realized that Grandpa Albert had snuck up behind him, quite unexpectedly. His grandfather was tall, lanky, gray-haired, bespectacled, and surprisingly quiet in his movements. He kept in shape, but his mind hadn't stayed as fit. Despite having an active intellect fed

126

by years of habitual reading, Grandpa Albert was beginning to fall prey to dementia. Daniel's mother and father had often talked about it at dinner.

But Daniel decided to answer his grandfather's question, and truthfully as well. "I was just looking at your old cedar chest, grandpa," he said.

"My old what?" said Grandpa, leaning in closer to Daniel. Grandpa's hearing was beginning to go too.

"Your old cedar chest," said Daniel, a little more loudly. "I was just looking at it."

"Oh, that old thing!" said Grandpa, laughing just a little. "Yes, I kind of wish I could put it up in its old place, though... somebody put a TV where it used to be. I watch that a lot, you know."

"Sure," said Daniel. He decided to change the subject. "How did you like the cake?"

Eventually, the birthday party began to wind down in the middle of the afternoon, and Daniel's various relatives and extended family, including his father's two brothers and two sisters, all began to leave with their families in tow. This to-do had been a big one.

As Daniel scrolled up and down on his phone in his spot in the back of his parents' car next to his sister Morgan, he dimly made out the conversation taking place between his mom and dad.

"He's getting worse every day, Jim," said Daniel's mom. "We need to put him in a home."

"I... I don't want to do that," said Daniel's dad. "He can still walk around well, and he knows what's going on. He's... he's just a little slow sometimes."

"He forgot what your name was!" said mom. "He's beginning

to forget that the place where he lives is called 'a house!'"

"It's not that bad!" said Daniel's dad. Daniel could tell that his father was trying to be patient. "Just... just... let's talk about it later, okay?"

When they got home, Daniel headed to his room to boot up his video games. But just as he was turning on the console, he heard a snatch of conversation coming from downstairs.

Daniel's primary job may have been playing video games, but he had just a hint of curiosity about things which didn't concern him, an element of his personality which picked that moment to surface.

So Daniel quietly turned off his video games, meandered over to the top of the stairs, sat down at the top, and listened to the conversation which was going on below.

"Okay, fine," his father was saying. "We'll... we'll work something out. Dad was smart enough to get his investments in order, and I know that he has something of a pot of gold hidden away. He had a living will written up, and I have his lawyer's contact info. I know that much. But he won't want to go into a home."

"We can't just let him live in that house by himself!" said mom. "If your brother won't let him move in with him, who will take him? Not Sue, that's for sure."

"Sue has a lot on her plate!" said dad. "And so does Frank!"

"Then why not put him in a home?" said mom.

"I... I don't want to do that," said dad. "And he won't like it either. I don't want to take away his... his freedom."

"Freedom to do what, exactly?" said mom. "Bumble about all day, not being able to make himself meals, and going out walking unsupervised, with no clue about where he's going or why? Because that's what's been happening since your mom died, and now it's gotten to the point where it can't be managed!"

The argument went on like that for a few more minutes before abating, after which Daniel heard his father migrate over to the living room where the TV was. The football game he wanted to watch would be on soon.

Daniel retreated back to his room, and the sliver of curiosity which had managed to worm its way to the top of his mind was beginning to grow, just a tiny, tiny bit. Grandpa had investments? Was he... wealthy? And what about that chest? Did that have anything to do with it? Or maybe it was just some kind of little joke or superstition that grandpa had?

Daniel knew that his grandpa had a reputation within the family for being something of an oddball character. Based on that, Daniel frankly wouldn't have been surprised if only the last of these questions could be answered with a solid "Yes."

But still... it would be nice to know what was in that chest. And if they were trying to write up a will, and grandpa had anything to give away in a will...

As Daniel sat back down in his room, he glanced around at his various worldly possessions. He had every installment of *Mass Effect*, *The Legend of Zelda*, and *Call of Duty*. There was his five-year-old flat-screen TV. His various game consoles, all lined up neatly in front of the flat-screen TV. What more could he want?

But then the words of Daniel's grandfather crawled out of that distant childhood memory of the cedar chest in his grandfather's study.

That is the bedrock of all my fortune and happiness. What's in that chest is something which everyone ought to have.

Daniel's eyes happened to glance at another item in his room.

It was a framed photo of Daniel and his family at Daniel's high school graduation. They had all been so happy that day. Daniel was going to go to community college, get his associates, and then go to a four-year college in Seattle and study accounting. He'd had it all planned out. And then... it just hadn't... it just hadn't worked out. He just didn't like college. No. He didn't.

But maybe... maybe I can try again, he thought. *I'll... I'll go to a real college. A real, four-year one. Out-of-state. And if grandpa... grandpa has money? He's... wealthy? I never... never would have thought... but...? But... maybe...*

He knew what he had to do.

Daniel's quarterlife crisis had been grating on him every single day since he'd turned twenty-five four months ago, and no amount of pressing buttons which allowed him to shoot digital bullets at digital terrorists was making that problem go away.

The course of action he was about to take was dramatic, but he was prepared for it. *I have to be*, he thought.

As his dad's football game was winding down, Daniel came up to him in the living room. The two were alone downstairs. Mom had gone to bed early.

"Dad?" said Daniel.

"Hey, Daniel," said Daniel's dad. Daniel's dad was pretty easygoing while unwinding, a trait which Daniel found to be rare in boomers.

"Um... is Grandpa Albert doing okay?" said Daniel. "I heard someone say something at the party earlier."

"Oh, we're just worried that Grandpa is getting a bit long in the tooth," said Daniel's dad. "We're going to need to do... to do something about that, I guess."

Daniel bit down. And then he bit the bullet.

"Dad," said Daniel, "I'd like to help out. And I have an idea about how I can."

* * *

Morgan was just as surprised as her and Daniel's parents had been when she had heard about the new job which Daniel now wanted to create for himself. "You're going to be grandpa's in-home caretaker?" she said.

"Yeah," said Daniel nonchalantly. "I have a driver's license, and I can drive grandma's old car to get back-and-forth between grandpa's house and his doctor's appointments and stuff." The two were loitering in the kitchen one evening after dinner. "Besides," said Daniel, "it's not exactly like I have anything better to do with my time."

Morgan didn't say anything, either good or bad. A gloomy girl with much better job prospects than Daniel, she didn't like college much more than he did. But as Daniel's mother was quick to point out, at least she was going to school at all, in addition to being gainfully employed as a front-desk receptionist at a health club.

"Hm," said Morgan. "Good for you." She then left the kitchen.

Three weeks later, Daniel had settled into his newly acquired role as his grandfather's in-home caretaker. His parents had been surprised, cautious even, but weren't about to question this sudden solution to a creeping problem.

"You can always let somebody else do it," Daniel's mother had said to him, in her gentle, gentle way. "It's great that you're volunteering for this big, big job, but we'll be right behind you every step of the way."

"Thank you, mom," said Daniel, who had taken a break from watching TV with grandpa. It was raining outside, and grandpa was still savvy enough to articulate that he wasn't inclined to go out in such weather.

Daniel saw his mother peer off to the side, before looking back up at him. Daniel had grown much taller than her over the years, but he still felt small in her presence.

Daniel's mother then said, "Just… just don't take on more than you can handle," she said. "I know you're trying to be helpful, but… don't… you know…"

"Relax, mom," said Daniel. He summoned every inch of charisma and charm that he had (which was very little), and spoke his reply. "I can do this," he said. "I… I can do this."

* * *

Daniel's daily routine as his grandfather's new in-home caretaker was equal parts simple and surreal. His father had warned him that old folks needed less sleep than not-so-old folks, leading them to wake up at odd hours. The result was that on one occasion, at three o'clock in the morning, when Daniel was still snoozing away in the meager guest bedroom he'd been afforded, he suddenly heard small noises coming from another part of the house.

Getting up and putting on his gym shorts, Daniel wandered out into the darkened, central area of the house where the kitchen was, only to find his grandfather pouring himself a bowl of cereal.

His grandfather didn't seem to notice him at first. But when a groggy, bleary-eyed Daniel came closer to him, Grandpa Albert looked up and said, in his croaky, strained voice, "Would you like some breakfast, Danny-boy?"

Daniel learned to take such behavior in stride, and he clumsily adapted to Grandpa Albert's eccentric routine. Grandpa would now wake up at four in the morning and eat some breakfast prepared by a sleepy Daniel. Then grandpa would watch the golf channel for a few hours.

But things would get really interesting in the middle of the morning on Fridays. At about that time, if it wasn't raining, grandpa would abruptly get up from watching the golf channel with Daniel, and shuffle over to the closet. The first time this happened, Daniel had been bemused as Grandpa Albert put on a sweater, coat, and baseball cap, and then turned to speak to Daniel.

"I'm... I'm just... going some place," said grandpa.

Daniel, who had gotten up from his spot on the sofa and had walked over to his grandfather, said to him, "...Eh, where are you going, grandpa?"

"Just... just out," said grandpa. It seemed that he'd began to lose his ability to speak almost overnight. He barely had enough presence of mind to put in his hearing aids and to put on his glasses.

"Do you want me to go with you?" asked Daniel. Even if his grandfather said "No," Daniel would have done everything in his power to follow along anyway. It was his only choice.

But grandpa never said "No."

"Sure, come along, Danny... Danny-boy," said grandpa.

Once Daniel had put on his own outdoor gear (they were solidly in jacket-weather at the time), he and grandpa went out.

They walked in the cold, still November air, the bright orange and yellow leaves of Fall covering up the ground around the trees planted along the sidewalks. Daniel kept pace with his grandfather, who still had something of a spring in his step, even at the age of ninety-five.

Their walk through the old suburb usually led them to a strip mall near the main road. Grandpa's house was only about a quarter mile from it, and Daniel didn't mind the exercise.

The destination of these Friday trips was a hole-in-the-wall burger joint. The first time that Daniel had bought some lunch there for him and his grandfather, he immediately realized why his grandpa was eager to come here. The burgers were the best he'd ever tasted.

The man who ran the store, a tubby, clean-shaven man known to Daniel as "Stuart," apparently knew Grandpa Albert as a regular at the burger joint.

"Yeah, he's come here like clockwork every Friday for the last six years," Stuart said to Daniel as they chatted over the counter. The burger joint, aptly called "Burger Central," was about the size of a campground outhouse, or at least the part containing the kitchen and dining room was. Daniel didn't have enough curiosity to wonder what the back of it looked like.

"Every Friday?" said Daniel. He glanced behind him at grandpa, who was still munching on his burger. How did the man look so fit despite periodically eating such grease-soaked meals? *It must be all the walking he does*, thought Daniel.

"Yep," said Stuart. "He and his wife used to come in together all the time, but then they stopped. But then he started coming back again."

"Wait… his wife?" asked Daniel. Stuart's last few words had now attracted Daniel's undivided attention.

"Yeah," said Stuart. "He and his wife, your grandma, I guess,

134

used to come in here all the time. I think they remembered it from when the guy I bought this place from ran it."

The cogs in Daniel's brain began to turn. "Um… how long did that guy own this place?" said Daniel.

"Heck if I know," said Stuart. "Old Bob was almost as old as Mister Albert is now when I took over this place a good fifteen years ago. It had a different name back then, and it was a pizza parlor."

Daniel glanced back at his grandfather. Grandpa Albert was just finishing up his burger, and drinking the last of his can of Coke. Was there something about this place which Grandpa Albert found magnetizing? Something that made him remember Grandma Nancy?

When Daniel and his grandfather finished lunch, they would walk back to the house and watch some more TV. Daniel would turn on the news sometimes, though his father had given them a Netflix account. Grandpa liked watching an old TV show on Netflix which Daniel had never heard of called "Columbo."

As Daniel sat back in the old sofa with his old grandfather in his old grandfather's old house, he kept playing over in his mind the years he'd spent not noticing Grandpa Albert at family picnics and barbeques. Could he have learned something from Grandpa if he'd given him more attention? Was there something going on in Grandpa Albert's mind, even now, that he ought to know?

He glanced at Grandpa Albert, who was still casually watching the news. A report about a local city council race was on. It was apparently in a dead heat. Not that Daniel had ever registered to vote.

Daniel's eyes narrowed, and he looked in the direction of his grandfather's study. He got up from his spot in front of the TV and gently walked over to the study. Grandpa Albert didn't seem to notice him leave. When Daniel came into the study, he approached the dusty, wooden chest which laid in the corner of the room.

What is in that thing? thought Daniel. *And if it's so important to grandpa... why doesn't he act like it?*

Just then, Daniel caught a hint of movement out of the corner of his eyes, and turned around quickly. Grandpa Albert was standing in the doorway of the study, smiling.

"Whatcha' doing there, Danny-boy?" said grandpa.

"Oh, I, uh… I was just seeing if the TV here was working," said Daniel.

Grandpa, still smiling, stared at Daniel for a few seconds, before bursting into a fit of snickering. He then left the room, saying cheerfully, "I guess that's good."

Daniel nodded, and decided to follow grandpa out, back to the living room. Perhaps it would be best to stay close to the old fellow.

A long afternoon of watching TV was followed by dinner in the evening, after which grandpa watched an episode of *Columbo*, before going to bed. After Daniel had made sure that grandpa was settled, he would go to his own room and go to sleep.

And that was what nearly every day was like for Daniel for the next two years. Grandpa and Daniel's mid-morning excursions to Burger Central on Fridays were complimented by grandpa's resolute tramping around the neighborhood on other days. Daniel went everywhere with him. He would see his parents on the weekends, when they came over to check on them to see how they were doing. Once in a blue moon, Morgan would come by. Daniel would drive grandpa to his doctor's appointments once or twice a week, and he would serve grandpa the dinners that mom made for them.

But Daniel had learned to cook a wide variety of foods himself. Mom came over one Saturday and coached him on how to properly make waffles, and later how to make lunches that weren't just peanut-butter-and-jelly sandwiches and potato chips.

"Those sorts of things are really bad for you anyway," mom would say as they made a nice salad together.

"I don't think they were meant to be anything else," Daniel said.

A day didn't go by where Daniel didn't think about what was in his grandfather's old cedar chest. But he gradually began to stop creeping over to his grandfather's old study to take a look at it. He had less reason to go there. He began to enjoy dining with grandpa, and the two managed to have basic, stilted conversations.

Grandpa's ability to speak was greatly limited by now, but Daniel was beginning to see that somewhere, in his grandfather's very soul, was a perfectly rational human being who simply couldn't get his faculty of speech to do what he wanted.

That theory of Daniel's was suddenly put to the test on a bright Sunday morning in the April of his third year of living with Grandpa Albert.

* * *

"I've… I've got to go, some… some place," Grandpa Albert said. Daniel watched him go over to the closet, like he usually did, and put his sweater, jacket, and baseball cap on. It was

137

a baseball cap marked with the insignia of a sporting goods company, a silhouette of a golfer. The hat was a new one which Daniel's dad had given Grandpa Albert as a birthday present last year.

What is it with old people and golf? thought Daniel. "Where do you need to go?" asked Daniel.

"I... I...," said grandpa, still putting on his coat. "I... I have to be... someplace. It's... it's... a day... which is... important."

Daniel furrowed his brow. *"Important?"* That was one of the few words he'd ever heard grandpa speak in the last three years which was more than one syllable long.

Daniel hadn't been idle during the last three years. After about six months of keeping an eye on grandpa, Daniel's father had convinced him to enroll in an online college. The tuition was cheap enough for Daniel's father, a sales manager at a glass manufacturing company, to pay for. Daniel, armed with a brand-new laptop, kept himself occupied doing that when not watching TV with Grandpa Albert. He'd be graduating in less than two years.

But who will keep an eye on grandpa then? he had often thought.

Now, it was April, and Daniel was still in the middle of studying for an exam in a supply chain management class. He had grown used to working on Sundays, but in the end, he had to justify to his father how he spent his abundant time. Daniel had quickly decided that online college was much more to his liking than regular college. Why commute to school, or even live on campus, walking from class-to-class and back to a dorm, lugging mountains of equipment, when you could do it all from the comfort of your dinner table?

As Daniel glossed over these matters in the back of his mind, his attention returned to his grandfather. Grandpa Albert was leaving the house, and Daniel quickly followed him.

As they walked through the suburb, grandpa took a new route, going in the opposite direction of Burger Central. Instead, Daniel found himself walking with grandpa to a very different establishment.

The sign in front of the building's packed parking lot read, "Bethlehem Lutheran Church." Daniel hadn't been to church regularly since he was fifteen, when his parents stopped making him and Morgan go. Eventually, neither of them kept going either.

But why was grandpa, who was now quietly shuffling through the front door of this small, wooden building with a steeple with a cross on top of it, going to church at all? What was special about this Sunday?

But then, Daniel heard the answer to his question in his ears, and he kicked himself for not knowing it. That answer came from the greeter who met him and grandpa at the door.

"It's great to see you!" said the smiling, middle-aged, mustachioed man who stood at the door of the church. "Happy Easter!"

Easter, thought Daniel. *Of course. Today's Easter. Grandpa... of all the things grandpa could have remembered... it was that.*

Daniel didn't know much about his grandfather's religious views, or even if he was particularly religious at all, even before he began to need Daniel's care. Again, Daniel had sadly paid little attention to him in social situations where the both of them were present. His Gameboy was just so much more interesting. At least, that's what he'd thought when he was a kid.

But now, Daniel found himself gingerly following his grandfather into the main room of Bethlehem Lutheran Church, sitting down with him in a back pew. It was nine o'clock in the morning.

The pastor, a stocky, happy-looking man in his forties with a mottled complexion and a thin beard, came to the front and introduced himself, before welcoming the churchgoers to the service and wishing them all a happy Easter.

"He is risen!" said the pastor.

"He is risen indeed!" replied the churchgoers.

The pastor, after a few more remarks, stepped down from the stage. A six-person choir, a forty-something woman playing a piano, plus a young man about Daniel's age playing a guitar, began to sing and play worship music.

Then, as the musicians played, as the choir sang, and as the churchgoers packing the small church sang along with the help of the printed-out lyrics sheets which had been placed in the pews, something incredible happened which left Daniel utterly flabbergasted.

Grandpa Albert, taking the papers in his hands, peered down at the words, and then began to sing.

"When peace... like a river... attendeth my way," sang grandpa, his voice rising with the rhythm of the choir, "when sorrows like sea billows roll... what... whatever... my lot... thou has taught... taught... taught me to say... it is... it is... it is well... with my soul."

Grandpa's voice stuttered and stumbled along with the rest of the singers, and the words he sang fell behind theirs. He followed along clumsily, and couldn't quite keep up. But he didn't stop singing, or at least stop trying to sing.

Daniel then realized that Grandpa Albert wasn't looking at the lyric sheets, not anymore. Getting into the middle of the next song (indicated in the lyric sheets as "Rock of Ages"), he slowly put down his copy of the lyrics sheet and sang on his own, looking ahead intently at the front of the church. A wooden cross was mounted in the center of the front wall, above the space where the choir and musicians were.

He knows the words by heart, thought Daniel. *This is all familiar to him. He... he knew that today was Easter. And... and I don't think anyone told him otherwise.*

The singing ended, after which grandpa and Daniel sat down with the other attendees. The well-built pastor then returned, and began preaching his sermon, where he expounded on chapter twenty of the Gospel of John. Daniel didn't catch the whole sermon, mainly because he was too busy keeping an eye on grandpa. Grandpa stared ahead, looking towards the front of the church, eyes glazed over and vacant.

Daniel's brain churned in thought. He had a million questions which he knew could not be answered. Was grandpa processing what the pastor said? Did grandpa, on some remote level, understand what the pastor was saying, or was at least trying to understand what he was saying? Had some kind of ingrained habit rooted in a happy memory from the distant past suddenly resurfaced in the form of going to church on Easter Sunday?

The forty-five minute sermon concluded. The pastor closed with a prayer, and the whole congregation bowed their heads, folded their hands, and closed their eyes, with grandpa doing the same.

Daniel wasn't sure if he ought to follow along. He was still trying to puzzle out the questions he had. But he wondered if he got an answer to at least a few of those questions when he saw a single tear fall down his grandfather's face as he bowed his elderly frame in prayer.

What's.... what's going on inside of grandpa's head? thought Daniel.

What... what is he thinking about?

Daniel bowed his head, folded his hands, and closed his eyes.

* * *

The hospital, Overlake Medical Center, where Grandpa Albert had been taken, was in Bellevue, across Lake Washington from Seattle. Daniel regularly drove his grandfather to a doctor's office near there. But now, Daniel travelled alone in his grandma's old car, a dingy Ford Cutlass. His grandfather had been given alternative transportation to the hospital.

Grandpa's physical health, as good as it was, had begun to degenerate over the last six months. He'd had trouble digesting food, and the doctor had prescribed more medicine and treatments. Grandpa's arthritis had gotten worse, meaning no more walks to either Burger Central or Bethlehem Lutheran Church. The latter of these had become another weekly destination for Daniel and Grandpa Albert, and Daniel couldn't say he disliked it.

But today, grandpa had abruptly collapsed onto the carpeted floor of the living room while getting up from watching the golf channel to get lunch. Daniel had just finished preparing homemade General Tso's chicken, the latest addition to his cooking repertoire. As Daniel drove along in his car toward the hospital in Bellevue, he thanked his lucky stars that he'd remembered to turn off the stove before calling 911, and then his parents.

An hour-and-a-half after grandpa had been picked up by

the paramedics and had been carried into the back of an ambulance, Daniel and his parents found themselves all sitting together in the courtesy chairs in the hospital lobby, waiting for the doctors to come back to give them a report on the situation. It was one-thirty in the afternoon on a Tuesday.

Daniel's father looked grim and stoic, sitting in his courtesy chair, blankly staring ahead. Daniel sat next to him, and Daniel's mother sat on the other side of her husband. None of them spoke, and they were all scared. None of them even had their phones out.

"I'm very proud of you, son," Daniel's father had told him earlier. "You've done so much, and you've come so far in the last few years. The… the whole family is proud of you. You know that, right?"

"Yes, sir," Daniel had said. "Thank you."

Finally, a doctor, a fit, balding man of perhaps fifty, came up to them. "He's stable," said the doctor, "but he'll have to stay at the hospital for observation for a few days. We may need to do an MRI."

"But he'll live?" said Daniel's father.

The doctor nodded, speaking kindly. "Yes," said the doctor. "It helps that he's in decent physical condition. He's got a bit of a paunch, but that's a lot more than can be said for a lot of ninety-eight-year-olds with arthritis and heart trouble. He's in good shape for a man his age, and in adequate shape for a human being."

"Can we see him?" said Daniel's father.

"You can," said the doctor. "He's sedated at the moment, but he'll be awake soon."

Daniel and his parents visited Grandpa Albert, who slowly woke up after an hour or so. He couldn't speak at all, and barely seemed to understand what was going on. When Daniel and his parents finally left the hospital at eight-thirty at night, he was sleeping soundly again.

As Daniel drove back to his grandfather's house, he struggled to concentrate on the road. Fear and grief gripped him. Was his grandfather finally going to pass away? Was he finally going to lose any chance he had of trying to understand what Grandpa was thinking as they went about their days together? Would he even be able to say goodbye?

Daniel had talked to his father about grandpa's weekly trips to Burger Central and his sudden desire to begin attending church. Daniel's father had little to say about the subject. As he drove down the highway, one conversation with his father came to mind. Daniel and his father had been sitting on the back porch of grandpa's house at the time.

"I know he grew up Lutheran," Daniel's father had said. "But he didn't stick to churchgoing for very long after all of his kids, including me, moved out of the house. I think both he and your Grandma Nancy began to think they were… above going to church, or… or something."

"Maybe… maybe he's trying to… get back in touch with his youth?" said Daniel. "I've heard that people with dementia or Alzheimer's, or… or whatever, I've heard that sometimes they remember things that happened a long time ago better than things that happened more recently. Maybe… maybe this has something to do with that kind of idea?"

Daniel's father had only sighed. "I don't know," he said. He sounded utterly glum. "I'm not a doctor."

Daniel finally arrived back at grandpa's house. He imagined that he'd wind up living in this house when grandpa passed away. Another cloud of melancholy descended on him as he opened the front door of the house. *Not "if,"* he thought. *When.* He walked down the front foyer of the house and toward the kitchen. He was by now intimately acquainted with the fact that this old house had a lot of memories in it. In spite of everything, Daniel got the impression from his extended family that those memories were mostly good ones.

Daniel walked back into the house's kitchen. He'd left all the lights on, and the door had been unlocked. He'd been in such a hurry to leave that he'd forgotten to lock it. The homemade General Tso's chicken was resting in a pan on top of the stove, now stone cold. Daniel went over to the sofa in front of the TV and sat down. The golf channel was still playing on the TV. Daniel then turned off the TV, leaned forward in his seat, and cried for thirty minutes.

After that, he threw the General Tso's chicken in the garbage and washed the pan. He preferred not to risk getting food poisoning. But out of the corner of his eye, he noted the gleam of the kitchen ceiling light reflecting on the shiny, gold-colored doorknob of Grandpa Albert's old study. Daniel walked over to the study, and opened the door.

The cedar chest was still resting in the corner of the room. Daniel, at the behest of his mother, periodically cleaned the house, which included dusting the study. The cedar chest had not escaped being dusted.

Now, at nine o'clock at night, in the old house which his grandfather had lived in for a good sixty-five years, Daniel went into the study, and turned on the light. The cedar chest was still there, shiny and clean.

Daniel approached the cedar chest, and put a hand on it. His hands stroked the surface of the chest.

But then he took his hand away.

No, he thought. *No. Not... not like this.*
He left the study and went to bed.

* * *

Grandpa Albert lingered on for a few weeks, but his condition only got worse. He had fought long and hard, but his battle was beginning to draw to a close.

Daniel was given the dubious honor of being invited to attend a family meeting, where his parents and his extended family began to discuss what to do now that Grandpa Albert could possibly be dying.

"He had a will worked out before Daniel had to come in to take care of him," Daniel's father said. "Dad had it all figured out, even then. He... he was always smart about stuff like that." The family had all gathered together in the spacious TV room at Daniel's parents' house. (Daniel didn't think of it as "his house" anymore.)

"I heard that Daniel started taking him to church," said Aunt Sue. "Do you think all that extra walking was the best thing for dad?"

"Sue, it was dad's idea to do that," said Daniel's father. He sounded testy. "Daniel said that dad wanted to go to church."

"I get that," said Aunt Sue, "but maybe we shouldn't have let him?"

"How were we, or Daniel... I... how were we supposed to stop dad from going to church?" said Daniel's father. His patience was wearing thin. "We couldn't have just locked him in his room!" said Daniel's father. "I honestly was just thankful that somewhere inside him, he had enough sense to stay at home when his arthritis got too bad! And since when is anyone going to church a bad thing?"

"If you think going to church is such a good thing," said Aunt Sue, "then why don't you go to church, Jim?"

"Why don't you go to church, Sue?"

The meeting went downhill from there, and Daniel happily allowed himself to shrink into the background while the argument among his relatives escalated. He had come to believe that silence was golden.

Eventually, the family meeting ended, and a decision was finally reached. Grandpa Albert would remain in the hospital, and the family would clear their schedules so that they could each spend as much time with him as they could. The doctors had said that there was only so much time left, and the one thing the family was united on was that they ought to enjoy what little time there was to be had with Grandpa Albert.

Days turned to weeks, and then it happened. Daniel was there, in Grandpa Albert's last moments. Every available family member was assembled, amounting to a collection of some fifteen people crammed into a hospital room the size of a large woodshed. Grandpa Albert was breathing in and out, slowly. The doctors and nurses had given them time alone. Nothing could hold back the inevitable.

"D... Danny-boy... come... come here, pl... please."

The occupants of the hospital room erupted in mumbling. But Daniel's father nodded to him, and Daniel came forward, to his grandfather's side. Grandpa Albert, weak and tired as he was, clearly had enough of his faculties about him to see Daniel one last time.

"I'm... I'm... pruh.... Pruh..." said Grandpa Albert.

"Grandpa?" said Daniel. He felt water welling up in his eyes. His throat felt like there was a golf-ball stuck in it.

"I'm pruh… per… per… per-ow…" grandpa said. But then he stopped speaking. Instead, he smiled, and said, with perfect clarity: "Well, you know."

Grandpa Albert then sank back into his bed, still smiling. After a few more seconds, his chest stopped moving up and down.

The room was silent for a moment. Daniel's nose was beginning to fill with mucus from his sudden fit of crying. Various members of his extended family were also shedding tears, and the room's silence was punctuated by such soft sobs. It was three o'clock in the afternoon, and it was Friday.

Eventually, Grandpa's body was taken away, and Daniel never saw his face again. As the family filtered out of the hospital, Daniel heard his father talking with Uncle Frank. Uncle Frank said to Daniel's father, "You know where he kept his will, right?"

"Yes, Frank," Daniel's father said, sounding drained. "In the upper drawer of his desk in his study. His lawyer has a copy, and there's another copy in his safe deposit box."

"And where's the key to his box?" said Uncle Frank.

"It's hanging on a peg at his house," said Daniel's father. "It's by the door, with his other keys."

Daniel just shook his head, and kept walking. He heard his mother talking to Aunt Sue about planning the memorial service. Aunt Sue said something about how to go about getting grandpa cremated.

But Daniel was lost in his own thoughts. *I'm going to get a look at what's in grandpa's cedar chest*, he thought. *Hip hip friggin' hurray.*

* * *

The reading of the will took place three weeks after the memorial service. The assembled family members were shocked.

"He left… he left all of his money to that church?" said Aunt Sue. "How come we didn't know about this?"

"Sue," said Daniel's father, who was present. His voice had become more weighted lately, and Daniel was beginning to think that such an occurrence wasn't altogether bad. "Don't make this harder than it has to be."

Aunt Sue opened her mouth to respond, but stopped. "Alright, alright," she said. "Just… just let Norm read the rest of the will."

Norm, who was the late Grandpa Albert's lawyer, sat taciturnly at the dinner table at Daniel's parents' house, around which the family was gathered. Daniel loitered behind the rest of the group, brooding in a corner. Grandpa Albert had been dead for a month. Daniel's father had asked him to deliver the eulogy at the memorial service, and Daniel agreed. He'd also requested some time off from his online college. When Daniel returned, he'd be starting the final year of his degree program. He'd have an accounting degree at the age of twenty-nine.

Daniel was then shaken out of his stupor when he realized that someone was saying his name. It was his father.

"Daniel?" said Daniel's father. "Did you hear what Norm just said?"

"I'm sorry?" said Daniel.

"Dad, I mean, your Grandpa Albert," said Daniel's father. "He left you something."

Daniel's heart suddenly leapt into his mouth. Was this it? He'd long since put behind him his vague plan of working his way into his grandfather's heart, and then into his will. Was this about the cedar chest? Thoughts about that particular knick-knack hadn't been occupying his mind in the midst of planning, attending, and recovering from the memorial service.

"Oh, uh, sorry," said Daniel, getting up from his seat and going to the front of the assembled relatives. "I wasn't paying attention, sir."

"Your grandfather," said Norm, "has left you a wooden chest found in his study, marked 'A.M.L.' That chest and everything in it is yours."

"He left me the house and the car," said Daniel's dad. "Everything else of value he had is to be sold and the money given to that church."

"Bethlehem Lutheran Church?" said Daniel. "The one which grandpa and I were going to all this time?"

"…Yes," said Daniel's dad. "Actually… that is the church that mom and dad went to with us when we were kids. It's… yeah, it's… it's been a while."

The meeting went on for a little while after that, before concluding around four o'clock in the afternoon. There was no end of grumbling and muttering among the grown-ups, though Daniel remembered that he himself was a grown-up now.

A week went by before Daniel worked up the courage to go back into his grandfather's study. His father had agreed to sell him the house for one dollar, and the car for another dollar, upon his graduation from college and acquisition of a job. It was a handshake deal.

"You've earned this, son," said Daniel's father. "I'm… I'm very, very proud of you."

"Yes, sir," said Daniel. "I… I… you've said that plenty. And

I'm glad to hear it. I… thanks."

Daniel was eating dinner with his parents and sister at his grandfather's house when his sister Morgan reminded him about the chest. Daniel had cooked up a meal of white-bean pork chili.

"Have you opened the chest yet?" said Morgan.

"I haven't," said Daniel. "But… why don't we all open it tonight? Now that we're all together?"

"That sounds like a nice idea," said Daniel's mom. "Jim?"

"I'm okay with that," said Daniel's father.

After dinner concluded, Daniel went over to grandpa's study and lifted the chest out of the corner of the room. It was about the size of a microwave, and it was heavy. Very heavy. Daniel needed the help of his father to lift it off of the ground and to carry it out of the study. "I didn't know dad had a brick collection," said Daniel's father as he strained to help Daniel carry the box into the living room.

But Daniel and his father managed to lug the cedar chest over to the now-cleared dinner table, and set the chest on top of it. His parents and Morgan stood around the chest. It had no lock on it, and sure enough, it was marked, "A.M.L."

"It's his initials," said Daniel's father. "'Albert Martin Laney.'"

Daniel nodded, flipped the latch which secured the box shut, and opened it.

Inside the chest were books. Piles of books, all at least twenty years old, all ranging in thickness from one to three inches. They had a wide variety of covers, some colorful, some a dull brown or black, a few paperbacked, some hardcover, and most leatherbound.

But they all had one thing in common.

"'Holy Bible?'" said Morgan, peering over Daniel's shoulder.

"What does it say on that one's cover?"

"Holy Bible," said Daniel, sifting through the pile of books, taking them out of the chest one at a time. And as he took each book out of the chest, he, with the help of his father, mother, and sister, soon were able to find what the chest contained.

"They're all Bibles," said Daniel, showing one to his father. "This one says 'NIV,' this one says 'NABRE,' another says... uh, it's a bit worn... 'NKJV'?"

"Looks like Grandpa Albert was a collector," said Daniel's father. Daniel's father got to the bottom of the chest full of Bibles, the tomes which the four were working to extract from the chest beginning to pile up on the table. There were easily more than four-dozen of them.

"But... why?" said Morgan. "Didn't grandpa... not go to church for a long time? And... are any of these worth any money?"

"I'm just as mystified as you," said Daniel's father. "Daniel? Can you shed any light on this?"

Daniel shrugged his shoulders. "When I was a kid," he said, "grandpa said I could have this cedar chest and everything in it if I wanted it. He said that what was in the chest was the source of his fortune in life. Maybe... maybe he just really loved God, even when he stopped going to church. Maybe he just... wanted to do religion on his own, and grandma did too. And then... maybe he just changed his mind near the end."

The four of them stood there, in the dining room of the old, cramped, but clean and neat house. The light of a warm summer evening shone through the windows, illuminating the dining room.

Finally, Daniel sighed heavily, and took the newest-looking Bible, marked "ESV," off of the pile that had accumulated on the table, before heading over to the sofa. The TV was off.

"What are you doing?" said Morgan. "Shouldn't we keep looking these over or something?"

"Maybe later," said Daniel. He sat down, and flipped open the Bible he was carrying. He knew what he had to do.

"I need…" said Daniel. "I need to catch up… on my reading."

19

The Sid Miber Killer

Day 1

Carpool to Spokane at first light of day
　　I, a young man, and two old dogs of war.
　　Discussed the Holy Bible on the way.
　　Will Caesar be on the convention floor?
　　Came to Spokane; Old churches next to banks.
　　Bums near the road; hotel is opulent.
　　Convention Hall; At lunch, no one gives thanks
　　To Christ the Lord, whose grace we all have spent.
　　Returned early to hotel; need to think
　　Outside the box, to help Rich Everett win
　　Yard signs for Sib Miber; The missing link?
　　Everett is a saint; Miber runs on his sin.
　　Election Night; Two-hundred nights away.
　　Will we trumpet? Or will the Donkey bray?

Day 2

Woke up alone in opulent hotel
  Woken by a strange radio; new sound.
  Convention hall the capitol of Hell;
  Is this Party dead? Buried in the ground?
  Pandemonium on convention floor
  Rules of this game do not make sense
  Miber is falling; Everett walked out the door
  Rich will not play; It is the best defense.
  Voted some more, we here in are clown cars
  Seated my PCOs in single row;
  Chair did not do his job, so we'll do ours;
  Did our business; I gave my friends a bow.
  Cheap Mexican food. With Young Party bucks.
  Decent boys, but they know naught of The Crux.

Day 3

Prayed with some others on the final day;
  "We pick a Caesar; we serve Christ the King."
  I, the young man, felt weak amidst the fray;
  Could only think of her I'd give a ring.
  But work had to be done, and so we did;
  Sat through endless motions and calls to vote
  My mind a boiling cauldron with no lid
  Stuffed my hands in the pockets of my coat.
  When all was said and done, I wish for friends

155

Thought I could find good cheer with strange young boys;
They speak of women as but means to ends,
They speak of girls as but living toys.
Tomorrow I carpool back home to see
If Washington is crazy, or just me.

Day 6

Returned home from Spokane with wise old men
    Miber was chosen, but that choice matters not.
    At home, my sister wept in sorrow, then
    I called after the Lioness I sought.
    Lioness gave me counsel; prayed for her.
    The GOP horse race, it counts for zip.
    We had some time apart, but now I'm sure
    From The Cup I'd gladly for her sip.
    We meet today, just to compare some notes
    The Lioness doesn't want to hunt with me.
    Miber; Everett; Don't know who will get the votes
    But Lioness, under the jungle tree?
    We may not hunt, but surely we can prowl;
    Walk together, in weather fair or foul.

Day 9

One week has passed since chaos in Spokane
    No word from Everett; want to have a Life.

Got an LD meeting I need to plan;
Know a woman I want to be my wife.
Comics! Audio! This small book of rhymes.
So many things I'd rather do than this.
Is politics the right thing for my times?
Want to learn, read, sing, go, woo, hold, and kiss.
Saturday: I go down to Auburn; South.
Make some friends; win some fans; Socialize.
It will be fun. Drive down there; Perform.
Can I yet make a living with my mouth?
Must plan May meeting; Call Everett campaign.
Win the race with fifty more doorbells rang.

Day 11

Life is good! But there's a coming night
   The distance, it feels like eternity
   My father thought he could help T. in his fight
   With a bumper sticker for Kennedy.
   I cannot put it off for much longer now
   Must help Everett; will no more lay about
   If he wins, can I take my final bow?
   If Everett wins, can I at last get out?
   A Republican Governor! The joy!
   It is a won'drous possibility
   I have hoped for it since I was a boy
   An elephant to make Washington free.
   The Lioness, returned from far away
   I obeyed her wish, for her soul to pray.

Day 14

Will send email! Plan meeting in May!
  Reach out to Everett! Aid him in his work.
  Lioness? Is it best to stay away?
  Go find green pastures where I can lurk?
  This month will be my holiday; Time off!
  Need to renew my life of prayer and book.
  Must remember, that beer, it is not froth
  And that the Sun is always worth a look.
  Off of Twitter! Onto the open road!
  Out on the lawns! Onto the Starry grass!
  Wind on my face takes no time to upload!
  The Sky is not walled off by screen of glass!
  Meditating on Second Chronicles,
  From it I divine noble principles.

20

Resignation

My duty is to lead a petty band
   In crusade against this age's spirit
   Our castle is but so much salt and sand;
   Our unsung song; Who would want to hear it?
   I chose this duty; but another quest
   Attracts me from the path of the crusade.
   Would finding happiness be for the best?
   Forsake the Elephant and tiger's blade?

Yet my sense of duty dares not to fade.
   Thought this sense of mine be put to the test,
   though tempted to retire to the shade;
   From warring with the Donkey I would rest.
   But for now, this war, I will not fear it.
   So long as I dwell in this gloomy land
   In crusade against this age's spirit
   The tiger's blade, I will keep it in my hand.

Far be it from me, to forsake my band!

For if I do not lead, who will command?

21

Evening

Shackled, chained, to the monument of flesh
  White mirror, portal to the painted Hell,
  My sins renewed, again so fresh;
  I long for holy, ghostly, churchly bell!
  This Palantir, it hypnotizes me,
  A vision; A parody of Heaven
  It numbs me, blinds me, to the mystery.
  Save me, Michael, you and all the Seven!

Can Bards and Poets same me from myself?
  Can philosophy save me from my sin?
  Will Iluvatar send some gentle elf?
  To guide me back to home and hearth and kin?
  Or will it take a mighty Lion's roar,
  Rending claws against my dragon's scales
  To break my craving for the Devil's door;
  Jesus, Mary, Joseph! Hear my wails!

If the mirror I cannot but abuse

I'll have no choice to it but never use.

22

Night

The Silver Mirror, White, bright, foul as bleach,
   The greatest tool of my magic spells,
   The methods of my magic it did teach,
   Opened the doorway to a thousand Hells!
   Hammer of Wonder! Yet, Cement of Death!
   Wizard's Wand, all-seeing Magic Mirror!
   Yet You alone gave Lazarus his breath.
   You'd laugh and ridicule my Palantir.

Can Devilish Hypnotism be undone?
   Block out by subtle tricks the evil lights?
   Or smash it all; forsake what can be won
   If it means winning my soul's daily fights.
   Put drapes over the Mirror? Blunt the Wand?
   Oh Aslan! Could I have no other choice?
   To forsake the cave where my magic dawned?
   Oh, to hear the Lion's commanding voice!

In the morning, I'll hear a cleric preach.

Oh, may I be as Simon on the beach!

23

Stewart

Part 1

The man named George, I cannot ever be;
   Kind, honest, brave, loyal George! In sum: Good.
   Just to wear his shoes and coat, that I would.
   But I am not George. I am only me,
   Am very unlike him most frequently.
   My spine is not of iron, but of wood
   I do not always do the things I should.
   To be as good as George is to be free.

Not, not like George; I'm not among the best.
   So I aspire to be good enough.
   But like old George, I am ordinary.
   And thought I don't stand tall above the rest,
   Perhaps I am a diamond in the rough.
   Oh! One day, may I deserve a Mary!

Part 2

Am I too old to go off over there?
   Or should I settle down in times of peace?
   Forsake desires for a Golden Fleece?
   My whole life, duty compelled me to share
   My neighbor's burdens, and I didn't dare
   To go off either to New York or Greece.
   The world, like some girl, seemed to tease
   me; sitting with my book in my armchair.

But times are better, indeed, times are good.
   My demons, great and small, have gone away.
   Wife, children, brother, mother, all secure.
   No, I am not old. Yes, perhaps I could
   go see the world gleaming in the day,
   now that, in time of peace, I'm free of fear.

24

Shimura

Part 1

Watanabe wasted his life away,
  Became almost a stranger to his son.
  When he saw that his life was almost done
  He had not instinct to kneel down and pray;
  He only feared here would be Hell to pay.
  But in his dying days, he went and won;
  Inspired many by what he had done
  Was mourned at night, and honored in the day.

Watanabe worked 'til he was old.
  I am young, and healthy, with many plans
  I do not wish to make my life a waste.
  In far off days when I am gray and old
  May I be famous, and with many fans,
  For this young man, he would the world taste.

Part 2

When a saint departs, what is there to do?
  Have a funeral; drink sake, and mourn
  the passing of a man so lowly born
  but who in death, just like that saintly Jew
  stood, campaigned, and lobbied for me and you.
  The hero lies in state; flowers adorn
  the shrine, where friends, their hearts all torn
  mourn the man who served when his days were few.

Could any man or woman be so great?
  Surely they, we, could at least aspire;
  Serve the people, like our departed friend,
  Who never had in him an ounce of hate
  and used the last flames of his dwindling fire
  to prove that men need not live Second-Rate.

25

Curtiz

Part 1

Rick the man lived a hard and honest life
   He was a man with many, many friends
   His honesty won him some dividends
   But his honesty kept him from a wife.
   Rick the man lived in hard times full of strife
   Devilish teeth, the human race it rends,
   Some to Heaven, other to Hell it sends.
   Rick the man took up not the butcher's knife.

Rick the man lived in tragic, grieving times;
   I, meanwhile, enjoy abundance Peace;
   If the times get hard, will I be like Rick?
   Will I refuse to commit any crimes?
   Even if my hardships only increase?
   To be a man, that is a magic trick.

Part 2

My friend, you see, gave up everything
   Forsook his wealth, his house, his woman too
   So that, to his conscience, he could be true
   even if misery would conscience bring.
   Oh, yes, how he wanted that wedding ring,
   How he'd have beaten blackguards black and blue,
   He might have even formed a gang or crew,
   For his love for her was so shattering.

But he gave her up, so that she could live!
   And even now, as I and my friend flee
   To go on some adventure far away,
   I see that lust takes. But love? Does it give!
   And whether my homeland stays slave or free
   I hope fortune repays my friend some day.

III

Bird Song

I am very, very proud of the sonnets included in this section. I actually like them, and think that a lot of them are kind of good. As for the short stories, I leave you, the reader, to pass judgment... but I really like 'em a lot.

26

Stranger

What to say to the stranger in the dark?
In a low-lit place, there is she and I;
Don't know if she wants me to live or die.
I don't know if my words leave any mark,
Or if I'm just a dog who didn't bark,
Or if I said something that made her cry,
And made her go chat up some other guy.
Maybe this stranger came here on a lark.

But if I see this stranger once again,
perhaps in yet another low-lit room,
I can start by asking about her day.
Let her know she's not in a lion's den,
that all girls just make me a baboon,
so just laugh off the foolish things I say.

27

J

Have I been looking for you all this time?
  Are you the one I dream about about at night?
  She's in the window in the Autumn light,
  She's looking for a man with whom she'll rhyme,
  Some cocktail where she can be a lime.
  But this girl and me are black and white,
  We are as separate as day and night,
  But I've been looking for her all this time!

Exactly who have I been looking for?
  A beauty for whom I can fight and die.
  It just wasn't until now that I knew
  The beauty whom I wanted to adore,
  That she'd just light up when I am nearby!
  You come alive when I am close to you.

28

This is My Blood

The world's artless, sleeping in the grave,
   It doesn't dream, for dreaming is to make.
   Dreaming done right, will cause the Earth to shake.
   A brilliant dream will salvage and will save
   the human race; by dreams they are forgave.
   Do you dream of the Lady in the Lake?
   When you dream, do you give or do you take?
   The Earth must dream! Don't hide yours in the cave.

The world's deathless, too much for my art;
   Far, green country; My fig tree and my vine.
   Dawn's rose red fingers, they come up to me,
   It calls my soul and gratifies my heart.
   "This is my blood;" and so I take the wine.
   And when I drink, I'm from the grave set free.

29

Long Winter

Oh, was there ever winter for so long?
  So many nights searching for better days.
  I contemplate the error of my ways,
  And try to figure out where I went wrong,
  But all I do is write this silly song.
  I am just lucky that for me it pays
  To write sonnets and ballads and some lays.
  My sword is brittle, but my pen is strong.

It is Winter, but I can pay the bills.
  I see Spring, and Summer is in style.
  Though what's in style may soon go away,
  I'll accept the times as the thing God wills,
  So I will be happy for a while.
  And then maybe happy every day.

30

Thurgood

Is there happiness to be found at home?
   Or is contentment on the open road?
   An airline ticket and no heavy load?
   Because I long to see some ocean foam,
   To tour London, Berlin, Greece, and Rome!
   I feel just like that fairy tale toad,
   Who got up and left his swampy abode,
   And found a princess far away from home!

To find the princess, you must be a prince,
   and princes do not sit at home all day.
   Princes go the distance on a great quest,
   Plunge into the depths, not just for a rinse,
   But in order to somehow save the day!
   Princesses like that about Princes best.

31

12/25

Is Twelve-Twenty-Five important to you?
   What is it that you do on Christmas morn?
   What does it mean that Jesus Christ is born?
   Does it matter than Mary was a Jew?
   Does Christmas Day mean anything to you?
   Does Twelve-Twenty-Five mean much in the morn?
   Is it just a day when red hats are worn,
   When someone you know sits down in a pew?

But if Twelve-Twenty-Five means anything,
   To folks in Bremerton and Bellevue too,
   It's about being happy when you're poor.
   Chief-of-State born in Section 8 Housing,
   To a teenage mom and blue-collar Jew,
   And now that kid is knocking at your door.

32

Carpe Diem

Mere mortals cannot see what is to come;
   The days to come are but a mystery,
   Dark as Sheol, bright as eternity.
   Will today begin with a battle drum?
   A trumpet call in Washington?
   Will the President sing an elegy?
   Will he intone a doomsday prophecy?
   No mortal man can see what is to come.

But in this ever-present fog-of-war,
   Where my lantern is but the flaming past,
   I let some other world fill my heart,
   And I let my mind guide me out the door.
   "Carpe diem!" And if this day's my last,
   I will simply make living life an art.

33

Bacon is Sexy

A coloring book with a picture of Spider-Man on it, and some brand new crayons.

That was my Easter present to Kiana Miller.

"Bacon is 6-E," said Chelsea as she instructed me on how to use the bacon fryer. She mashed the buttons swiftly, precisely. Two motions. "See? Remember it this way. Bacon is *sexy*. Got that, Eli?"

I nodded. "Yes, ma'am," I said.

Chelsea grinned. "I'm not a 'ma'am,'" she said sweetly. She turned and started walking away, surprisingly swift and agile despite having a few extra pounds. "Hang on a sec, Eli," she said, "I need to go to the back of the store for a minute."

I nodded. *Hm. Smoker.*

I had been working at Burger Central (not the real name of the restaurant) for about 3 weeks. I'd started by operating the broiler. Then they had me move boxes and clean floors with a mop. Now, Chelsea, the assistant manager, was teaching me how to cook bacon. Which was (like Chelsea) "sexy."

Did I need the job? Not really, but I was done with high

school, college sucked, and I wanted something to do. When I sat down for my interview with Kyle, the General Manager, he looked a little bored, but also slightly amused by my intense politeness and my clean buttoned-up shirt.

"When can you start?" he said.

I thought for a moment. "Would next Monday be okay?" I said carefully.

He grinned and chuckled. "Time of day, kid," he said. "What time of day can you start working?"

"Oh, uh…" Was he offering a job? I'd never been employed by anyone other than my dad before, so… "Um, would 7 AM be okay?" I thought for a minute. Eight hours a day, so… "…and work until 3 PM?"

Kyle nodded. "Sure. That would be great."

So I started working. I got free food, and I always ate salad and water. Just trying to be a good little boy.

After about 4 months there, I met Kiana Miller (not her real name).

Kiana and I often had our ten-minute break at the same time. I would sit down in the break room, and read a book, and she would pop in, sit down, sip her coffee, and stare at her phone.

I would glance over at her occasionally during these ten-minute moments of working-class fellowship. She was smiling at her phone, which had some pictures on it. She snickered. "He's so cute," she muttered to herself.

I couldn't help it. "What's up?" I said.

"Just my kid," she said. "He's at daycare right now."

I nodded. "You have a kid?"

"Two kids," she said. She got up from her chair, and put her phone away. "Two little boys," she said, "just them and their mom against the world."

She walked out of the break room.

I sat there. I still had 3 minutes left on my break.

How... how old is she? Like... Twenties? Maybe thirties? I... gosh, she's just so tiny. Two kids?

I worked at Burger Central for nine months, and I got to know Kiana pretty well. She was on welfare, lived in a subsidized apartment, wanted to be an actress, wore glasses because she couldn't afford contact lenses anymore, and she really, really hated being poor.

"Jesus, y'all," she would say as she worked the line, assembling burgers, while I scrubbed the counter on the other side, "I'm getting out of this place ASAP."

"Sure," said Kyle as he worked next to her.

"I'm telling you," said Kiana, "I've just got cast in this big show. I'm gonna totally be on TV."

"Mmhmm."

"Yeah, yeah, I'll send you pictures and everything."

I rolled my eyes, smiled a little, and said nothing. John Le Carre once wrote that the lower the pay at a job, the more interesting your coworkers are.

I frowned later as I scrubbed dishes in the sink.

How much does Kiana even get paid? Is it enough to afford basic needs for those two kids she has?

One time, Kiana and I sort of talked about this when we were sitting in the break room together.

"Gosh, if Trumpo gets elected, our country is ska-*rewed*," she said as she was staring at the phone. I think this was in 2015.

I peered over. "Why do you say that?" I said.

She shook her head, not looking up at me. "Well, I mean, he's a Republican," she said. "Those guys always wanna cut welfare. Cut the minimum wage, cut this, cut that…" She shook her head. "Why can't we have people at the top who wanna *grow* things?"

I felt very sad suddenly.

Surely I could offer a solution?

I cleared my throat. "Well, I mean, a higher minimum wage could mean that people like us could lose our jobs, Kiana."

She stopped looking at her phone, and slowly looked at me. "Huh?" she said. She looked like I had just swapped places with some kind of alien creature.

I felt my face go red. "Well, I mean, a higher minimum wage drives up the cost of labor for the owners of restaurant chains like Burger Central, so if the minimum wage goes *up*, there will be fewer jobs. I... well, it's just... economics. That's all."

She nodded. Her mouth was open slightly. She shook her head, put her phone away, and got up. "My ten's done," she said. She left the break room.

I sat there.

Dear God in Heaven, why did I say that?

But Kiana didn't hold grudges. Thirty minutes later, we were both yucking it up after somebody (it might have been me) made a stupid joke about one of the other employees being on drugs or something.

Easter came. I'd be leaving the job soon. I had enough money.

But... my conscience was bothering me. Maybe it was my scripture readings that day. Something about the sheep and the goats. Of helping other people in need being the same thing as helping Jesus. I don't know. I don't.

My father was driving me home one day. I had a plan. I'd seen something on Facebook Marketplace. I wanted to get it.

"Yeah, it's over there," I said, pointing to the house which had been listed in the Facebook Marketplace ad.

"Here?" he said.

"Yeah, here." It was a free listing. I didn't have to pay anything.

I jumped out of the car, wearing a jacket over my Burger Central uniform. It was really hot out.

I was greeted by the owner of the ad, and I scooped up the item: An old, barely-used coloring book with a picture of Spider-Man on it.

I smiled. *Every kid loves Spider-Man.*

A little later, I walked over to Fred Meyer, and paid perhaps eight dollars for some brand new crayons.

Monday.

Kiana and I were cleaning up in the breakroom. She was putting on her coat, and I was rooting around in my backpack. We were about to both go home. She usually left while I was taking my second 10 minute break.

"Okay, adios!" she said.

"Wait, Kiana?" I said.

"Yeah?" she said, not looking up. She was beginning to dig out her phone.

I scooped my gift out of my backpack. "I have something for you," I said. I had her full attention. I handed her the coloring book and the crayons. "Happy Easter. This is for your kids."

Kiana deftly accepted the book, but she just stood there for a few seconds. Her eyes went wide, her jaw dropped open. She gasped. She then looked up at me, and smiled the loveliest smile I'd ever seen. She had beautiful teeth. "Oh, Eli…" she said. "I… this is so sweet…"

I just smiled back. "I was just thinking of you when I saw it. That's all."

She beamed, nodded, and walked out of the break room.

When my 10-minute break ended two minutes later, Kiana was still in the kitchen. She was talking to Chelsea, Kyle, and some others.

"-and he got me this!" she said. She looked really excited and animated. "My kid is going to love this! This is so cool! I can't believe it! Look at this! Look!"

She then left the restaurant, while I just stood there, at the broiler, smiling.

* * *

"Ha ha ha ha ha! See, that's why I love you, Eli."

* * *

I never saw Kiana again after I left Burger Central.

Somehow, I friended her on Facebook. A couple Easters later, I was scrolling through my feed, and I saw a post from her. It was a picture of a bunch of ladies at a black church or something walking around in colorful, pink dresses.

I looked at Kiana's profile picture. I winced. She was dressed in lingerie and posing in a lewd manner. In her Facebook profile.

I looked at her Facebook information. *Current City: Los Angeles, CA.*

I shook my head. *Kiana, I... where are you really?*

I looked at my contacts. Kiana was online.

I shook my head. *God, I... why does this happen to people?*

I typed a note to Kiana.

Hey, Kiana. My family is having a get-together for Easter next week. My mom said I could invite a friend if I wanted. I don't know if you're in town or not, but you're more than welcome to come.

A few minutes later:

HIII eli!!!! Ya, I'm, like, totally slammed right now. Rly wanna come, but, well, y'know. WORK. Thx for asking, tho. ;)

There were a bunch of heart emojis after that message.

I rolled back my swivel chair, and stared at my shoes.

Who... who is the father of those two kids you have Kiana? Did... whoever that guy is... did he ever buy them a coloring book? Did he ever buy them anything?

I got up from my chair, and walked upstairs. I wanted to go sit in church and pray for some reason.

Easter came, and I was shoveling roast beef into my mouth. My mother came up to me.

"Hey, Eli?"

I swallowed a bite of broccoli salad. "Yeah, mom?"

"Most of the guests have already arrived. Is that girl you invited coming? Uh… LaDa or something?"

The color drained from my face.

Current City: Los Angeles, CA.

I lost my appetite.

"Uh, no, no, she… uh, she had plans. Yeah. I just forgot to tell you earlier."

"Oh, okay. No worries. Don't forget to try the carrot cake!"

"Thanks."

I sometimes still wonder if Kiana's kid is in high school right now.

34

Mocktails

"Dancing Queen" – Written by Benny Andersson, Björn Ulvaeus, and Stig Anderson – Performed by ABBA – Courtesy of Polar Music, Epic Records, and Atlantic Records.

* * *

Abby turned down the car radio. Her car was a beater, but she liked it. She had just turned 21.

Her mom had rolled her eyes when she said she was going to a club.

Mom, I'm an adult now. I'm gonna go do adult things. When I get back home, I'll say, "Mission Accomplished." Toodles!

North Seattle. She was on her way to the club which her sister had told her about. *Blue/Red Fix.*

It was legit, classy. Not sketch.

There! A parking spot! Thank heaven. It was really late for her, but, well, she wanted to go out.

She was wearing an old hoodie. Her glasses were still on. She hoped her hair still looked good underneath the gray cloth.

She'd spent a while styling it.

As she parked near the club, she glimpsed, in her peripheral vision, her book bag. Her books were there.

Salsa. Hip-Hop. Swing. Flamenco.

They were really great books. Some had never been published.

Her mom was a gymnastics instructor. A champion. Almost went to the Olympics in the '80s.

Her mom, 2021: *Abby, I... of course not! I... I think you're special! Your talent is genetic for all I know! Sweetheart, I just don't want you to waste your... talents. I... Abby, I...*

Now:

Abby winced. She saw herself scrunch up her face in her rearview mirror. She remembered what she, Abby, had said, in 2021. It was her birthday for God's sake.

She had thoughts: *Yikes, Smithouser. I mean... why? Abby, you... that... that probably cut pretty deep, even then.*

She shook her head.

Okay, okay, she thought. *No books. No... it's real this time. Let's do it.*

Abby walked through the club. The music was loud, but not ear-splitting. Cool, but not overbearing. Tracks were a mix of oldies and contemporary.

She'd taken off her glasses and put them in her book bag, leaving it in the car. She could see okay.

Okay. LFG, people. Yaaaaay...

It was a good club. Lighting was perfect.

Abby went over to the bar.

Abby sat down at the bar. She hated the taste of alcohol. Just... ick. She liked music, and she liked parties, and she kind-of-sort-of-well-I-guess liked clubs, but... Yeah. Mocktail, please.

She felt a bit tense. She saw other kids... *adults...* getting carded.

Youareanadultyouareanadultyoudanadultorderadrinkforpetessa ekabbyugh...

One lady bartender who was supervising the other servers immediately saw her. She saw Abby just sitting there, not getting carded. Abby was wearing her "battle dress." Not a party dress, *battle dress.* Custom black jeans, special black shoes from New York, black wife-beater, even. Her hair looked great. She was a natural blonde.

The lady bartender, very pretty, forties, dark hair, came up to her, smiling. She had a tattoo on her forearm, with some kind of rose logo on, with text that read: *Blue/Red Fix.*

Abby at first thought the woman would tell her to leave. But instead, the lady bartender ducked under the counter, rooted around in a minifridge, and came back up with a bottle of chilled water. She gave it to Abby. No charge. Big smile.

Lady bartender's lips moved: *Yeah, I know the type. Mocktails, right? Hope this works.*

Abby grinned. *Good omen,* she thought.

She was on the dance floor. The next song was about to start. Abby was getting ready.

Her thoughts: *Ten...* eleven *years of lessons... first time doing it at a club... Oh, look, mirrors...*

Okay. GO!

The DJ turned up the volume of the song a bit.

Boom.

Spin. Turn. Footwork. Pirouette. MOVE, GURL!

On the edge of the dance floor, a wallflower named DeShawn (he had a tie on) lounged with his friend Luis. He saw Abby.

He whispered to Luis. Luis shrugged.

DeShawn nodded appreciatively. *What... Gee... she has a clear path to the DJ table... I... Holy-*

Single, Double, *Triple* backflip, backward somersault...

Her thoughts: *ithinkicanithinkicanithinkicani-*

Applause!

DeShawn grinned for the first time that night. Feet first on the DJ table! *Girl! Woof, that was a... I heard that* wham *happen! Whoo!*

His thoughts: *Jeez, even my mom couldn't have done that. In her prime! I... who* is *that?*

And then...

Only one way to find out. Let's go, Mr. Lopez-Brown. Be a grown-up already. It's time.

Abby extended her arms, spreading her hands out, just like that one lady on the back of her favorite CD. Everyone in the club had seen her. Some were pumping their fists, others were cheering, their cries inaudible against the loud music. A few had their hands over their mouths and were whispering to their girlfriends, gasping.

Abby smiled brightly. She could read one woman's lips: *Tiffany, who is that girl? I haven't seen her at Fix before.*

DeShawn stepped up onto the DJ table. He had good footwork. Abby saw him. Her hands were still extended.

Oh, um, a guy, uh... hi.

She was still grinning. It was a real grin. She looked at the guy.

Abby's last boyfriend (she was 14, he was... *yeah*) was...

...a BIG. *Jerk.* He, like, worked at a casino. Aye yi yi... So. Embarrassing.

DeShawn casually, gently took her left hand. Abby let him.

190

He kissed her hand. He was smiling. He had good teeth.

Hm. Never got that *from Ryan. Classy, mate.*

Her thoughts: *Well, um... okay. I... Oh, hell. Why not?*

Boom.

He was great! His footwork was amazing. Great moves. Salsa. Swing. Hip hop. Flamenco! Good!

Wait. Wait. WTF-?!

What... what was that... the *tango?* How... how does he know... *I* don't know the tango! I'm barely keeping up! Wow, I...

He *had* to have had training. How could he *not* have had training?

How old was this guy anyway?

In the Manager's Office at Blue/Red Fix, Bryan, the club owner, was looking over some balance sheets. Business was good. His door was open. The loud music helped him concentrate on his work.

We was wearing reading glasses. His sleeves were rolled up. He had a tattoo on his forearm with a rose symbol from his old rock band on it, with the text *Blue/Red Fix.*

Gina walked in. Her tattoo matched his.

He could hear her okay. He read her lips, anyway: *Bryan! Come look at this! There's these great kids on the floor! C'mon!*

Bryan and Gina leaned on the balcony together. Bryan nodded. Lots of memories. Gee, those kids right there, they...

He narrowed his eyes. He smiled a little.

He whispered something in Gina's ear.

"Gina, you know that's Kate Smithouser's kid right there, right? Doesn't Kate's other kid run AA with you at your church?"

She gasped, put a hand over her mouth, smiled, then gave him a big side hug.

"Oh, so you do listen to me, Blue."

His name was DeShawn Lopez-Brown. He was 22.

Abby and DeShawn were sitting at a random bus stop (no park benches available) looking at Abby's Flamenco book. Abby was pointing at one picture. *That was totally you! You did that move! Number 4! You have absolutely had training! Don't tell me...*

DeShawn just shook his head. Smiling. *No. No training. I swear.*

Abby couldn't stop laughing. But then...

Rats. Contacts fell out on the way here. Must have been when I was washing up in the bathroom.

I... Uh...

She reached into her book bag, and fished around for her glasses. Oh, um, would he... mind?

Ryan *did* mind. He hadn't liked the braces either. Ugh. *High School.*

She put her glasses back on. She looked at DeShawn. Sheepish grin. Um...

DeShawn was still smiling. He reached into his inside pocket, pulled out a pair of orange, plastic glasses, and put them on.

We're two of a kind, Abby. Promise. I'm just some guy from Kirkland. I like MTV. And I like you too.

And then:

Uh... heh, I... that's honestly the first time I've ever been in a club. I went to a private school. Yeah. Also, my mom is Kat Lopez. Yes, that Kat Lopez. Yes, from Broadway.

Abby gasped. Hand over her mouth. Laughing. O. M. G!

She grabbed his hand, and swinging the connection back and forth, they started walking up the brightly lit, newly finished sidewalk, books forgotten. There were fireworks lighting up the sky. It was New Year's Eve. Day. New Year's Day. Happy New Year, Abby.

Him: *So...! Wanna get mocktails, princess?*

Her: *Hahahahahahaha... "Princess?" DeShawn, dude!*

Her thoughts: *This is great.*

She felt like she was a kid.

1 Year Later:

"It's nice to meet you, DeShawn. Your mom was on Broadway? Neat! Abby just... she can't shut up about you! Great to have you over on Xmas! I'm Abby's mom, Kate. Make yourself at home!"

35

Juice

"Blue Boy" – Written by Boudleaux Bryant – Performed by Jim Reeves – Courtesy of RCA Records.

* * *

They were in the break room at work. Aaron had just said the wrong thing to Claire. The unspeakable.

Aaron: *You're beautiful.*

He was a college dropout.

Claire: *Um, yeah, Aaron, uh... I like you, but... can we talk for a second?*

They had a phone call on a Tuesday morning.

Aaron: *So... you're saying... it's a "It's not you, it's me" kind of thing?*

Claire: *Aaron, I... Ugh. I'm just saying, maybe we need some time apart. It was kind of fun, but... I just want to be friends. Okay?*

He stopped in at the shop where she worked. It was busy, but she saw him immediately. She had a new job.

Claire: *Oh! Hey Aaron! What's up, bro?*

Aaron: *Oh, hey Claire. It's, uh, it's great. I'm trying college again.*

Claire: *Awesome! I'm proud of you!*

Then *he* walked in. Claire lit up like a firefly.

Claire: *Hey, Franco! Where have you been? I missed you!*

Franco: *Claire! Wazzup, girl?*

She came out from behind the counter. They hugged. Aaron left.

"Okay, everyone, welcome to Marketing 214, I'm Professor Wall, spelt like it sounds, W-A-L-L, and *no*, I did *not* vote for Trump, I don't care about politics really, this is Advertising, for God's sake…"

Aaron was sitting next to a very pretty girl named Jessica. She was really smart. Kind of like… Claire.

Claire wasn't very pretty, but Aaron thought she was smarter than Jessica.

Before: *"You're beautiful."*

Aaron winced. *I take that back*, he thought. *Claire is much prettier than Jessica.*

But, well…

Aaron turned to Jessica. "Hey, Jessica. I'm Aaron? Marketing 102?"

Jessica had been staring at her phone. Aaron thought she was watching an anime. The lecture was starting. Jessica took a lot of notes, but she seemed indifferent.

Jessica noticed Aaron. "Oh! Hey Aaron! Um…" She stopped smiling.

Jessica knew that look. Intimately.

"Aaron, um… I'm gay."

Aaron: *Um… Oh.*

Aaron sat in a park, drinking a glass bottle of Coca-Cola he'd bought at a taco shack. It was his day off.

He'd come here with Claire on Christmas Eve last year, before she'd started seeing Franco, because neither of them had anything better to do. It had been fun.

He drank from the Coke. It tasted good.

Three years passed.

Aaron was actually pretty good at school. Just needed the right motivation. He had some money now.

Summer. One more year, and he'd graduate.

He was walking by the shop where Claire worked. He thought he could see her at the counter through the front window. He tried to remember… how long had it been since… the break up? He wasn't sure what to call it. They weren't dating, really. Just… friends.

He glanced through the shop window at random and saw… Franco?

Franco and Claire looked like they were having a big, animated argument. Aaron couldn't hear anything, and he decided to just keep walking.

About a block away from the shop, he heard the door of the shop slam open, and he noted Franco storm out, walk up the sidewalk, overtake him, pass him without saying anything, and turn around the corner ahead.

Aaron's thoughts: *Oh, um, well… I guess that was… Franco.*

Yeah.

Aaron walked back to his car, a reliable beater from 2002. He liked it, took care of it. It got the job done. He got into the car, started it, and drove home.

His thoughts: *Um... yeah. I think I'll lay low for a while.*

Claire sat in her mom's living room. Franco was gone. She was more bored than drained, really. Franco had a great body, but, well... he worked at a car wash, and he never remembered her birthday, and he hated all the food and movies she loved, and he laughed whenever she tried to tell him about a rough day, and...

She went to her room, got her cell phone, and went through her digital photos.

She found it.

The picture: Her and Aaron, Christmas Eve, that park.

Her mouth twitched involuntarily.

Claire: *Why do you want to take a picture of us, Aaron?*

Aaron: *Well, it's just... I thought today was really nice... and I want a souvenir. I... want to remember this.*

Claire: *...Um, here. Let me take the picture. I'll send you a copy. But... you do NOT show it to anyone.*

Aaron: *Promise.*

She sighed. Why had she talked that crossly to him? He never spoke like that to her.

Claire remembered something just then.

Aaron (Before): *"So... you're saying... it's a 'It's not you, it's me' kind of thing?"*

She rolled her eyes. *Well... I dunno*, she thought. *Maybe you're right, mom...*

She'd seen Aaron since this picture had been taken. He'd lost a lot of weight.

She looked down. *Um, yeah, weight loss...*

Aaron had never cared about that. Franco wouldn't shut up about it.

Claire cracked a smile. She looked at the picture again. She grinned.

Her thoughts: *Fine, you win, you big kind-of-unemployed dope.*

Ring. Ring. Ring.

Aaron: *Um, hello? Aaron speaking.*

Claire: *Um, hey! Yeah, it's me. Uh... do you wanna get... juice or something?*

36

My Name is Jim

"I Ain't Got No Home" – *Written and performed by Woody Guthrie* – *Released on Dust Bowl Ballads (1940)* – *Courtesy of Victor Records.*

* * *

Jim was on vacation. His wife and kids were at the beach. He felt a little tired from the drive.

He sat at the dining table in the hotel room, sitting at his laptop. He typed a little in a Word Doc.

He was almost 70. He didn't feel all that old.

Hm, he thought. *Well... how did it all get started, anyway?*

One year ago.

Jim sat at his favorite greasy spoon downtown. He usually came with his son Eli (aged 29, late bloomer, at community college now), but he came alone this time. He was hungry.

"Hey, Jim," said the waitress. Jim thought her name was

Sandra or something. She was a blonde, about his wife's age. "Eggs and hashbrowns again? Wheat toast?"

"Sure. Thanks."

There was a TV playing on the wall. Jim forgot whether it was MSNBC or CBS. It was a news report about Gaza or something. Screaming kids. Jim winced.

I hope Sandra turns on ESPN or something. There's a Mariners game on tonight, I think.

Jim was talking on the phone with a cop from SeaTac. His older brother, Ed, had just had a rough day.

"Look, officer, I get that his license plate was expired, yes, but... my brother is more than 70 years old! Did you really need to take him to the station? He's pretty lucid, honestly!"

Some kind of mumbling. Jim thought he was talking to a woman. He didn't care, honestly.

"Look, thanks for understanding," said Jim. "Just... take care of yourself, okay?"

More mumbling.

Jim hung up.

I wonder if the Mayor of SeaTac is a red or a blue, he thought.

Jim was talking on the phone to another cop. This one was from Kent.

"Yeah, thank you, yeah... yeah. I understand. Yes. Thanks officer. God bless. Thanks."

Jim hung up the phone. He was at work. The family business.

His office assistant walked into the room. Jim knew that Eli had a crush on her. He didn't approve, but Jim kept quiet.

"Hey, Jim. Everything alright?"

Jim shook his head. He didn't know how to feel.

"My sister, um... yeah, Lisa, yeah. She's... she's gone. Heart attack. She was doing really well for a few years, but well... she smoked a lot, is all."

Jim's office assistant was about 23 years old. She had red hair and was named Christie. She looked awful.

"Jim... that really bites. I'm sorry."

Hm, thought Jim. *Maybe I should cut Christie more slack.*

Jim was at the bank, waiting for an appointment. He was reading the *Times.* He thought this edition was from yesterday, maybe last week.

There was this one headline: *Mayor of SeaTac arrested Monday Night; 4 charges filed.*

Jim shook his head, and gently set the newspaper aside. The story sounded kind of gross.

Jim actually didn't really like the news, but he was bored.

His banker came out of the back office. It was 9:30 AM, Monday morning. It was summer. It was beautiful out. Lovely weather. It was August.

"Hey, Jim. Appointment?"

Jim got up. "Hey, Carrie. I'm ready, yeah."

Jim didn't get the loan.

Another appointment at the bank. November. A week before Thanksgiving. Jim liked how the election had turned out.

It was Carrie again. Carrie's boss sat in the corner, on a courtesy chair. He looked bored.

"Um, Jim," said Carrie, "I get that your business did better than last year, and, yes, you are very good, very consistent at paying off debt, but well... you just have a *lot* of debt. I..."

Carrie shook her head. "Jim, well... do you have any... collateral?"

Jim sighed. "I... well..."

Jim got home. It wasn't that late, but he felt tired.

Thinking about money made him feel old.

His wife was on the sofa, scrolling on her phone.

"Hey, Jim," said Jim's wife. Her name was Nancy. "How was work?"

"Oh, um... it was fine," said Jim. "Um... how was the appointment with the... uh... dentist?"

"It was a mammogram. I did fine. Just routine. Nothing wrong!" She was smiling. Nancy loved playing Wordle.

Jim nodded. *Thank you, Jesus,* he thought to himself.

Nancy used to have arthritis in her hands, but she got a shot or something. She ran a couple of marathons every year.

Jim was talking to Mitch, a... friend. It was Christmas Eve. Eli was in the corner, drinking a Coke.

Mitch's wife and Jim's wife were friends. They had met at a Zumba class.

"Yeah, we just retired. Got a house out in... Bremerton," said Mitch. He was smiling. He had a really clean shirt.

Jim nodded. "Great," he said. He wanted to change the subject. "Uh... so, read any good books lately?"

Mitch shook his head. "Jake Tapper is putting out this new

book in, like May of next year or something. It's about Biden. Just something I heard from a friend in New York on a Zoom call last night, I…" Mitch drank some kind of red liquid. It might have been Port.

Mitch muttered something like, "What a bastard."

Jim pretended not to hear that. It was Christmas.

Valentine's Day.

Jim had a date planned with Nancy, but Nancy was feeling tired. She'd been at work today. Eli was sitting at the kitchen table, drinking a Dr. Pepper. Eli was doing very well at community college.

Jim glanced over at Eli. He looked bored.

Christie had quit yesterday. She had gotten a new job at a law firm down the street. Jim hoped she was happy.

Eli shook the can of Dr. Pepper. It was empty.

Jim and Eli were visiting Jim's daughter (Eli's sister) Rachel at her dorm at the UW. Rachel wanted to be a doctor. The whole family was proud. She was 22. She had talked about a scholarship or something. Grad school or Med school, one of those two. Really high GPA.

After lunch, they walked back to the parking lot. On the way, about 200 feet away, Jim saw a bunch of pro-Gaza protesters getting arrested by some cops. He thought he saw a dumpster burning somewhere. His hearing wasn't as good as it used to be, but he thought he heard some kid scream something like "F the Jews!" or… yeah.

Jim hated swearing.

When they got to the car, Eli buckled up in the front seat. He was graduating in about two years.

Eli shook his head. "Lovely people in this town, y'know?"

Jim didn't say anything. Eli's favorite professor was Jewish. The family was Christian.

Vacation. May 2025.

Jim sat in front of the laptop. He thought for a long time. *Where... where did it all start? For... for me? What is my story, anyway?*

Eli was studying marketing at college, but Jim knew that Eli wanted to be a writer. Jim was sad. He didn't know anything about writing. He ran a light manufacturing shop. Eli was miserable whenever he came down to work there. Being a few offices over from Christie probably just made things worse. And now even Christie was gone.

Jim had visited his mother, Eli's grandmother, in her assisted living facility a week before Jim and his family left on vacation.

Hey mom. Uh... can I talk to you for a minute?

Sure, Jim. What's on your mind?

Well... you ran that newspaper back in White Center, is all, yeah, I mean, I know that, but... well... can you tell me a little bit about... writing?

Hm. Well, whaddya wanna know?

They talked for a long time.

Jim drove home. On the radio, there was this old Woody Guthrie song playing. Jim liked it.

At the hotel, Jim starred at the Word Doc. He hadn't typed anything. It has been 2 or 3 minutes since he sat down. *Hm.*

Well... what was that one thing mom said? Um... yeah, that's right. "*Start at the beginning, finish at the end.*"

Francine Jane "Fran" Ionello-Swenson had won a bunch of awards for her old columns back in the '70s. She was 95 now. Eli loved her.

Jim sighed. Well... the beginning...

He began typing.

Hello. My name is Jim. Nobody knows this, but I voted for the Libertarian guy last year. I forget his name, but... yeah. Now you know something about me.

He cracked a rare smile.

Yeah. It's a start.

He hoped Eli liked it when it was done.

37

Castro

*"And You Know That" – Written and performed by Kenny G –
Released on Duotones (1986) – Courtesy of Arista Records.*

* * *

MKTG 249. Advertising.

Eli sat in the front row. It was early. Hardly anyone was there. Even the professor wasn't there yet. It was an evening class.

He really, *really* liked marketing.

He had his notebook out. Pen. He was ready. He was doing okay in school. It was springtime.

Castro walked into the class. She had dark, swarthy skin, her face was covered with acne, her dark hair was in a messy, frizzy bun, her sweater was old and tattered, like it had been washed too many times, she wore gray sweatpants, and her shoes were perfect.

She sat down in the front row, right next to Eli. She got out a pen and a little notebook, and looked at the blank whiteboard.

206

At this point, Eli hadn't met her before, so he didn't even know her name at the time.

Eli just thought he should introduce himself.

"Um… hello. I'm Eli, Eli Swenson. Nice to meet you."

The woman who had her face covered in acne (It actually wasn't that bad. Eli actually thought it was attractive. Later that night, he decided she actually looked like the world's most beautiful porcupine.) slowly turned her head in Eli's direction, like she was tired and sluggish. Maybe she was.

Her lips expanded in a lovely smile. Enticing. She didn't show her teeth. Her face was resting in her left hand.

"Castro," she said. "I'm Castro."

Eli nodded. "Oh, um, well… is that your first name or your last name?"

"My last name."

Eli turned back to the front of the class, slowly. The professor, a man whose last name was Kent, had arrived.

I guess she prefers last names.

"Hey everyone, I'm Jason Kent, Professor Kent, call me Jason, please, this is Advertising, welcome, welcome…"

Two hours later, class was over.

Castro got up to leave. She packed up her bag.

Eli put on his baseball cap. "Nice to meet you. Castro."

Castro looked at him. She smiled. Eli saw her teeth this time. "Thanks. Bye, Eli."

Oh. So… she's okay with first names?

Castro walked out of the classroom. She moved slowly, but like she was a ballerina or a dancer or something, conserving her energy. Eli wasn't sure if it was polite to try and guess her exact weight.

What… what is her first name anyway?

Friday.

It was late. He'd gotten all his work done. He'd remembered. The class roster. Everyone in the class could see it.

Hm, thought Eli. *Lucy.* Lucy *Castro. Lucy... I... I like that name. It's like the girl from Narnia.*

Castro's student profile on the class page didn't have any other information. There was a profile picture though, featuring Castro (or "Lucy," Eli supposed) all dolled up with makeup that hid her acne, and she was wearing lipstick. In the picture, her hair was dyed blonde.

Eli frowned.

Y'know what, Lucy? I like the real *you better.*

Two years passed.

"Hey, Castro."

"Hey, Castro!"

"How's it going, Castro?"

"Great job in that work group, Castro. Thanks!"

"Woof, way to go, *Castro.* You saved this group's ass!"

Lucy Castro laughed at that one. They were in a video chat at the time with their work group. "Um, thanks, Eli, but, uh... please don't swear, I just... well... I don't think it's... professional?"

Eli beamed.

"Sorry, Castro."

New Year's Eve. He called her on the *wrong* night:

Um... yeah, sorry, Eli, but... no. I... no. I've gotta lot going on right now, just... yeah. I... yeah. You're great but... no. Sorry.

But...

Castro didn't avoid him. She seemed to enjoy his company. She was never sad when he was nearby.

They both decided to join the speech club. Professor Jason Kent ran that club.

"Okay, you two," said Jason (he insisted they call him "Jason." Eli thought he was kind of irritating, honestly), as Eli and Castro sat in his office. "I... well. You're quite a team. Eli, your writing, presentation, and delivery, and Lucy, um, your research and planning and slides... you're basically the dynamic duo. Um..."

Jason leaned forward. "How do you two feel like going to a tournament? Maybe in..."

Eli leaned forward. *New York? Miami? Santa Monica, maybe? I know we do international trips sometimes, so... I dunno... Paris?*

Jason grinned. "Detroit! The big-wigs got a really good deal for the convention center there this year!"

Eli hadn't been smiling, but now he was disappointed. "Um... well..."

Castro nodded. She was grinning, ear-to-ear. "I would love that, Jason!" she said. "That sounds exciting!"

Eli quickly said, "Yeah! I'm in!"

Detroit.

Jason was giving them a tour of the convention center.

"Yeah, Detroit has really turned around recently. Third lowest crime rate in the Midwest these days!" said Jason, gesturing toward the gleaming, brand new convention center where the tournament was going to be.

Castro beamed. "That's amazing!" she said.

So are you, thought Eli. He cracked a smile.

Eli and Castro were in the hotel lobby, late at night before the convention, practicing. Jason was sitting in a chair nearby, scrolling on his phone.

"Don't forget the data!" lectured Castro. "Stop leaning on quotations so much! I know you like poetry, but-"

"I've got this, Castro!" said Eli. "Don't worry! We've got this in the bag!"

Castro started to object, but then she smiled. That enticing smile. "Alright... Swenson," she said.

Jason looked up from his phone. Before Eli could say anything, Jason got up and said, "Alright, Eli, Lucy, let's call it a night. We've got this, we've got this."

As Eli was chaperoned back to his room by Jason, he grimaced.

Eli's thoughts: *Crap, he knows everything. This guy has seen things. Clever SOB New Yorker.*

"We won!" said Castro. She was grinning! God, Eli loved that acne.

They were in a... juice shack. Jason's idea.

"Cheers, guys!" said Jason.

Eli smiled through barred teeth. *Why is he here, again? It's not like we're minors or something.*

Oh well. At least Castro looked happy.

Jason elbowed Eli. "Hey! That song playing on the speakers!

210

That's totally Kenny G!"

Eli eyed Castro knowingly as he downed a glass of strawberry-carrot juice. Yum.

I wonder if Jason is too old to be my best man or something. He's not so bad, actually. He set this up right?

God! He totally knows I love... um... Oh.

Senior Year. June. Finals Week OVER.

Overheard at Graduation, Commencement Ceremony after-party:

I'm really proud of you, Eli, but, well... Lucy is my student too. Just... be careful when you decide what it is you want.

I... Jason... have you ever loved a woman?

...Eli, buddy... I'm divorced. And I'm Gen X. I've seen things... I... Sure. Go get her. Be young. Good luck.

Eli and Castro were carpooling from a networking event in Edmonds. It had been a bust. But they were having a big talk. It had been Kent's idea for them to go.

Eli's thoughts: *Psh. "Job fair," indeed. Nice one, Kent. You clever bastard. God, I love you man...*

Girl you really really turn me on...

"Um, yeah! I love Narnia! You... ha ha... you honestly thought you'd have time to read a book at the mixer, Swenson?"

"Well, I, y'know..."WHAM.

The car flipped over, did a flip, and landed on the side of the road, in somebody's field. Wheels down, perfectly safe, even safely in park.

Eli Swenson was terrified.

"Castro! Castro! Castro!"

And then:

211

"Lucy!"

Lucy Castro was a bit dazed, but honestly more confused by Eli's reaction than by the near-fatal car accident. There had been, like, a freak pothole or something, and...

Lucy Castro, slowly, like a... very scared little girl, turned to Eli. To "Swenson."

"Eli... how do you know what my first name is?"

Eli turned to her. He suddenly realized they were both holding onto each other's shoulders.

How... how do you not know? How could I not know? Of... of course I know! I know you, Castro! And you know me! You know that I... you know!

His thoughts: *Oh, hell.*

He kissed her. She kissed back.

They did it again after a few seconds.

They walked up the highway, hand-in-hand, not speaking to each other.

Eli's cell phone had been busted up in the crash. Castro's was out of juice.

Eli looked at Castro. She was staring ahead. Even her blank, placid, neutral, resting expression somehow looked like a seductive, coy smirk. He loved that.

Last summer, he had surprised her with a video chat, where he revealed that he spoke perfect Spanish. He had been practicing for two summers. She laughed. She was in her home country, visiting. She was in her old room, for the first time in years. The video chat's background wasn't blurred out.

Swenson, I'm Brazilian. My native language is Portuguese.

Eli stared into the video chat. He felt like he was going to throw up all over his Lenovo laptop.

But then Castro had giggled. *But... you're sweet. And I also speak fluent Spanish! Psych!*

After a big laugh, they talked until midnight, PST. In Spanish.

He learned so much about her. Things she could never tell him before, because she just didn't have the words.

Castro was different after that night. So was Eli.

He understood so much after that night. There was so much that suddenly made sense. She... she did care about him. She just...

In Spanish: Yeah, my dad, my grandad... I dunno. I just have issues, Eli. Big issues. I... I'm not very good at... this.

The road.

It was dusk. They were still holding hands. They had left their coats in the car. Her arms were bare. Her blouse had been torn by something in the crash, ruined... and she was wearing a thick, cheap, polyester tank-top beneath it.

Her hair had been styled, but now it was matted, sweaty. Dark, frizzy... real.

She looked beautiful. She'd always looked beautiful. This was the *real* Lucy!

"Lucy... what about us?" said Eli. "I... I love you... Lucy."

Castro- *Lucy*... looked drained. She didn't smile.

And then, one word, from Lucy. One word: "Burgers?"

Eli nodded. "There's a McDonalds, in like, a mile."

Lucy turned to Eli, slowly.

She *was* a dancer.

She had done gymnastics in high school (she was a regional

champion, actually), back in that unpronounceable but very romantic-sounding city she was born in ("Gosh! It's not... it's not... it's a garbage dump, Swenson! Sheesh!"), and which he wanted to go back to with her, some day, *any* day, to talk to her father, in Spanish, about... things.

She grinned. The acne made her look like her face was decorated with gold stars.

Her: "And I love you too."

"Alright, here are your boarding passes. I hope you and Mrs. Castro-Swenson enjoy your... honeymoon, in Costa Rica! You are free to board."

38

True Story, Part 1 : Deep Breath

"I'll Never Get Out of This World Alive" – *Written by Hank Williams and Fred Rose* – *Performed by Hank Williams* – *Released in 1952* – *Courtesy of MGM Records.*

* * *

Her name was Letty Lung. She was 19. Her parents were Chinese, but she wished more people asked, honestly. *That* conversation would be more interesting than... this.

She. Was. Reallyreallyreallytired UGH...

SOC 101. Professor X.

(Literally. That was what she called herself. Her first name was Xochitl or something.)

ECON 202. Office Hours. Professor Mackey.

"Um, yeah, Letty," said Dr. Mackey (she knew he was a Ph.D because she read his bio on the college website). "I get that you're attending all the classes, and doing all the homework *on time*, getting all the tests done *on time*, and taking lots of handwritten notes, and watching all the videos, and going to the tutoring center at least once a week, and reading extra books from the college library about stuff we discussed in class, and reading books *I* prescribed on the Syllabus as supplemental readings, that's all *great*, but…"

Letty felt like screaming. This man was supposed to be a faculty chair. Why was his office located next to a random elevator near the Public Safety Office? She felt claustrophobic. The curtains were ugly.

Dr. Mackey leaned forward. He was trying to be empathetic. "…well, why are you getting a 1.5 in my class? It's like you're not even trying, but, well… on paper at least, you're doing gr…"

She felt her left eye twitch. She didn't need glasses. She had 20/20 vision. She could have gone to nationals for kickboxing, but she thought playing soccer would help her make more friends. It didn't work out that way.

Ugh.

Finally, she snapped.

Well… sort of.

"Um… Dr. Mackey… maybe it has something to do with the fact that you canceled 55% of all in-person classes, all with less than an hour's notice, then had the test prep class moved to a week before the exam instead of a fortnight, then it was canceled after 30 minutes when it was supposed to be 2 hours after only 8 people out of 30 showed up… and you made your teaching assistant run it? Who majored in music?"

Dr. Mackey blinked in bafflement.

Letty's expression was bored. That wasn't far off from how she felt.

Her thoughts: *Former Microsofter. His brain is fried from spending 12 hours a day staring at Excel sheets on an Apple laptop for 10 years before going on meds and getting a teaching gig at Green River.*

Dr. Mackey nodded. He had that weird, upside-down smile smart people put on when they realize somebody they know nothing about is smarter than them, and that this strange person could spit on them if they wanted to.

She got a B.

Her dad really, really wanted her to get an A.

"Study hard, Letty dear," he said at dinner, smiling. "I believe in you."

Prof. Mackey doesn't, thought Letty as she shoveled home-made macaroni and cheese into her mouth. *Maybe he will one day if I ever interview him for a job opening.*

Saturday. Letty's day off. She was talking on the phone with a friend from soccer.

A "friend." She was at Harvard Law right now.

"Yeah, so there, was this, um, guy last night, and well, I dunno, Letty, I just... I remember you, you were really cool, and this guy is just, wow, I... Letty uh... you're a Mormon, right?"

You wanted to have a Zoom call, begged me to pencil you in for a cell phone chat, constantly texted me for two weeks about "something BIG", and... you have boy trouble.

"Brooklyn, my dear," said Letty sweetly, "I'd love to tell you how you could absolutely charm that nice, dashing, new-money scion from Utah who wasn't even drinking anything at the mixer you went to, and I think I have lots of ideas... but didn't you say in one of your texts that your tort exam prep paper, which was, like, 35% of your final grade, is due at 11:59 PM? EST?"

Silence.

Then:

"Omigosh Letty I how did you remember my exam oh shi-"

Letty cut her off. She looked (and sounded) bored: "I am a nondenominational Evangelical Christian, you bimbo! *Protestant!*"

Click.

Letty slammed her smartphone on the kitchen counter and walked away.

Thanks for that letter of recommendation you never wrote, Miss Star Goalie. I hope your dad has enough money to pay for summer school, if they have *that. Good luck with that scholarship. Careful not to get caught doping or something.*

She went into her room and screamed into a pillow.

Letty wasn't known for being mean, sarcastic, or anything but good good good, perfect perfect perfect, Christian Christian Christian, sweet sweet sweet...

But...

...that's *easy* when *nobody cares* that you got an "A+" in AP Chemistry when 60% of the class failed their attendance scores, and maybe, like, 10% got a B-, at the highest, and you *still* never got invited to be the student guest at that faculty conference the teacher wasn't shutting up about.

She was best friends with this one girl who got a higher grade than her. That girl had joined the military. Letty missed Juanita. A lot.

Letty was out to breakfast with her dad. His name was Fang, but he went by "Tony."

Her thoughts: *Why don't you just make people call you "Fang?" Those DEI people at corporate would fall in love with you. You even look like an action hero, dad! Stop trying to be boring! You're not!*

Dad was wearing a clean shirt and tie (not his very clean shirt, he wore the older one when at Lenny's Cafe, in case of grease stains), and he managed to look cool even when he was wearing smart-people glasses. Letty thought her mom said something in Chinese while a bit tipsy on rice wine last New Year's, something like, "Fang! This is just like that party downtown back in..."

Letty couldn't do Chinese. Her one blind spot.

Dad leaned forward. "Why Biola, Letty?" he said. He was very kind.

Letty tried to do that smart-people upside-down grin... didn't work. She knew dad was smarter than her.

Why not be honest?

Letty opted for puppy dog eyes. Wrong move. "Dad, I'm lonely at Green River," she said. "Everyone there is really, really mean, and I-"

Dad shook his head slowly. He put a reassuring hand on her shoulder. She immediately felt better.

"Perseverance, my brave, warrior princess," he said calmly.

She wanted to cry. She loved it when he said that.

"Okay, daddy."

Letty was in the Student Counseling Office. She'd called her dad before they brought her here.

"Look, for the fourth time, I do not have mania, depression, or anxiety," she said. "I am just kind of irritated. Being kind of upset and stressed is *not* a psychosis. I don't know why Prof Cosgrove is freaking out. Doesn't he have any emotional intelligence? He's a faculty chair, Dr. Rufo! He's been doing this for literally four decades! Hasn't he ever had a student who tried debating abortion?"

Dr. Rufo sighed heavily. Out of the corner of her eye, Letty noticed a diploma on his wall.

Her thoughts: *Washington State University. Huh. You're pretty athletic, Rufo. Did you get into your Psy.D. program because of your SAT scores, or because you were good at kicking a polyester ball? Does WSU even take the SAT anymore? I wanna know. Really.*

"Um, Letty, Professor Cosgrove has a very stressful job, and, well, you need to cut Bob some slack…

GAH. WHY PHIL 101? Why not Comm Studies?

"He started it," said Letty, biting out her "Ts." "I want to call my dad. Give me my phone *now.*"

Letty was sitting in the waiting room. She could hear her dad lecturing Dr. Rufo down the hall. In Spanish.

Letty smirked. *I know Spanish. And dad doesn't know I know Spanish. I'm almost fluent. He's proficient, but…*

She heard *everything.*

"…and Andrew, my very, very fine friend, if you *ever* speak that way to my daughter, or to any of her friends, boy or girl, *ever* again, I will tell the board of his college some very unfortunate information about your resume. Securities fraud is very different from what you are hiding, but your slip-ups over the past decade are much, much easier to prove, and frankly, far more embarrassing. Stay away from my daughter, you little emaciated shit. You might want to try vacationing in Mexico... again. Permanently. Early retirement could be *very* therapeutic, my dear boy."

Wow.

And then:

Maybe my little smart mouth is genetic. I wonder what's really on his mind when he talks Cantonese on the phone with that deadbeat uncle of his from Hong Kong?

Dad took her by the hand, and they walked out to the car. It was, like, 4 PM on a Thursday. The campus was deserted.

"Let's go get steaks," he said, not smiling. "I'm starving."

I never want to leave home, honestly. I wish homeschooling had a Ph.D program.

They were at Nordstrom. 7 PM. The steaks were amazing.

"Work ethic is important," said Dad as they walked out to the car. They were both carrying a bunch of boxes. He was wearing his best suit. "Self-respect is about three levels up on the practicum. I want you to start dressing like a professional. It's not enough to act like one. You have to look like one."

She grinned. *Oh, um... Armani. He... what is Dad's net worth again?*

Dad shook his head. "Don't get too excited. Green River has the best Applied Accounting program on the West Coast. All the smartest junior associates at my firm studied there, and half the partners took remedial classes there too. I believe in you. I also want you to believe in yourself. Don't forget to buckle up, Letty."

Letty grinned ear-to-ear, and shook her head. *Mom sometimes leaves their tax returns on the kitchen table. I... yeah. I'll keep walking if I see them there... this year. Again.*

Saturday. Another day off.

Letty was reading a book. *Confessions* by St. Augustine. She'd never read it before. She'd just settled down, and turned to the introduction, when...

Her dad walked by. He was in his PJs. It was... sort-of... early. He stopped, bent down, and picked something up.

"Hm," he said. "What a nice penny."

He got up, put it in his pocket, and walked away.

Letty was tired. They had been up late last night making sure all the clothes were up-to-code. Dad had great... fashion sense. For men. And women... kind of. Mom hated the clothes he'd bought her. She thought she heard them arguing in Chinese when she was trying to sleep at like... 1.

Letty kept trying to read. *I wonder how many pennies he's stuffed in his sweatpants over the last 55 years? I want to get him a birthday gift. Any birthday gift. Any. Thing.*

Mom won. Dad was banned from buying clothes for his daughter. Letty didn't need to know Chinese to get *that.*

She was going out to her car to go to school in the morning, and she saw her mother watering the plants. Her name was Jessica. She was, like, 40. She used to be a dentist.

"Letty, darling," said Jessica sweetly, "your father thinks all non-lawyers are insane. Don't believe him. I don't know what job you will get after you're done with college, but whatever it is, you'll make *enough.* Your father understands now."

She smiled serenely.

222

Letty sighed heavily. Her backpack was heavy. *Mom, I basically agree, but... I wish I was James Bond, not Betty Crocker.*

Time to go to school.

"I'm so proud of you for that A+ you got in Philosophy," said mom sweetly.

Letty stopped dead.

Wut... tha... FU-

She ran to her mother, hugged her very tightly, and cried into her pink shirt for 8 minutes.

Fall Quarter. It was her... second year.

MKTG... SOMETH- what-the-sorry-dad-I-don't-usually-swear-I'm-just-having-a-bad

It was PR. "Extra Credit." From Grandmaster Fang. He and mom both liked the idea.

Letty had wanted to major in Physics. Her father hated academia. So did she. But...

> *I want to take summer classes so I can graduate faster.*
> *Letty, no.*
> *Why! I hate my li-*
> *Stop. Letty Lung. Stop. Now. Please. Trust. Me. I love you. You know that! Warriors are patient. That is how they win.*

Letty was in the back of the class. She usually sat in the front, but... that had been Phil 101.

Warrior, huh? Well... what about princess? Where's Prince

Charming when you need one? Dear Jesus, can you please stop making me keep dating my da-?!

A very handsome young man sat down right next to her. He had a baseball cap decorated with the Chinese flag. He was white as Joe Biden, but with better hair. He looked a bit older than the average college student. Late bloomer, maybe?

"Hey, Lung," he said, in a bland Seattle accent. "Nice job in that batso Phil 101 class last Spring. So, PR, huh?"

Letty had a deer-in-the-headlights look. She wasn't bored.

"Uh… I'm sorry, but… what's your name again?" she said after about 2 minutes.

The young man didn't smile. He was busy getting out a pen and paper. He and Letty were the only ones in the class not taking notes on laptops. They looked like… non-cheap pens. They were from Staples.

"Charles," he said blandly. "Charles Irish. I'm not Irish. It's a long story, but I'm Scandinavian."

Uh…

* * *

1 Year Later:

So, Charles, my fine young friend, your sister is a missionary in Taiwan? Oh! Uh… Yes. Yes, I understand. Yes, your Cantonese is excellent, by the way. I know Letty has been studying it on the sly using YouTube, and she is standing at the door of my office even now- Oh? I… well. Yes, yes, I know. What? Why? Why no boyfriends? Are you serious, Irish? She's a rabid junkyard dog! She sends all her crushes fleeing for a nice safe Soviet gulag! Why don't... oh, uh... yes. I... yes. Steak. Of course. I'm sorry. I was being... inconsiderate. Yes, I... yes. Yes, a movie. She loves Scorsese. Yes. Um... bye. Yes, please, take a deep breath, *I... okay. Um... yes... cheerio.*

Letty was wearing her favorite dress. She heard everything. She grinned. She started jumping up and down in the foyer like she was six years old.

She screamed:

"Gotcha, Fang! He got it on tape!"

39

True Story, Part 2: Irish

"Englishman in New York" – *Written and performed by Sting* – *Released on Nothing Like the Sun (1987)* – *Courtesy of A&M Records.*

* * *

> *Hey, Letty here.*
> *I should probably explain what's going on.*
> *Charlie doesn't think his story is interesting,*
> *but whoever is reading this,*
> *Do. NOT. Believe him.*
> *- L.I.*

And now, back to our regularly scheduled program...
BEEP

* * *

Chuckie Irish had schizophrenia.

Maybe. Sort of. Who knows. Certainly not... Doctor? Doctor... Tereshenko? She... she was an... an MD, right? Uh...

He'd been diagnosed, like, 8 years before he met Letty. He was about 21 then. Bye bye, Divinity School scholarship.

The following conversation happened 1 year ago:

"Yes, yes, you were put on several different medications when you were in the hospital in 2017, Chuckie," said Tereshenko, in a thick Russian accent. She had a giant floral picture on her office wall. Chuckie's family was not poor, just cash-strapped. He was on state insurance. His mother was sitting in a courtesy chair outside Tereshenko's office. The clinic was in Tukwila.

"Dr. Tereshenko," said Chuckie patiently (his parents called him Chuckie. He wasn't sure what he wanted to call himself. Not "Mr. Irish." Nobody even called his *dad* that), "I understand that my symptoms as described by my mother on the phone are... very alarming, but... I feel great. I... those new meds from Cordello, the nurse practitioner, are working! I get that my behavior has been different, but... I feel different!"

Tereshenko looked at him like she had just met a turtle who could discuss dialectical materialism. In Latin. He later found out her foreign Ph.D was in Cultural Studies or something. She was an NP too, actually.

She said: "Chuckie, do you know about Klonopin?"

His thoughts: *Please God help me to... remember the Golden Rule.*

After sorting out how to manage his meds, Charles Irish got a new therapist with legitimate credentials, and then moved on. He was tired of being "sick" all the time.

Sometime Later:

He and Letty got coffee after they first met. She... said "Yes" very quickly.

"Why Philadelphia?" said Letty. "It's... kind of random."

Charles (not Chuckie, *Charles*) shrugged. "I like M. Night Shyamalan. I dunno. Maybe I thought I would try running into him at a hoagie shack near wherever they have 76ers games. I just needed to get out. Spring Break was great."

Letty's smile curved... upward. Incrementally. Almost imperceptibly.

Charles wore glasses. He read a *lot* of books.

"I really loved *Unbreakable*," she said quietly.

Cool, thought Charles Irish. *Netflix?*

Letty snickered, and pushed back her long, black hair. To him, her hair looked like very, very dark-blue plants, growing near a quiet, misty spring, somewhere in England. He was a poet.

"Yeah..." she said, since he hadn't said anything. "Dad... he's a movie buff. He used to own the DVD."

Charles Irish grinned. His thoughts: *Oh... you're different, Ms. Lung. Like... me?*

They started seeing each other. Just to talk about "homework." And to talk about... everything else.

"Psych ward?" said Letty. She and Irish (she called him "Irish") were sitting on a stone lift outside one of the campus buildings, drinking black coffee. It was a gloomy October afternoon. Their books and backpacks were piled on the grass nearby.

"Yeah," said Charles, or Irish. "My doctors *still* won't give me a straight answer when I ask for a diagnosis. I... it feels like they're *trying* to keep me in the dark about it so they have an excuse to keep me drugged up."

Letty shrugged. "Maybe the reason they aren't giving you a specific, textbook diagnosis is because your condition isn't extreme enough to merit one."

Irish turned to look at Letty. "I'm sorry?"

"You're doing pretty great, Irish," said Letty. "You're not dangerous, I mean. I'm not afraid of you. You're probably the most normal person I've ever met at Green River, to be frank."

Irish felt his face morph into a big smile. Letty smiled back. His thoughts: *I... I like you. I...*

I love you.

Charles Irish lived with his Aunt and Uncle. Irish didn't get along well with his parents.

But...

He called them on his birthday. Just... to be nice.

"Yeah, Letty is great," said Irish. He was talking to his mother. "Um... because she is rational? And intelligent? And really mature for her age? And... we have a lot in common...? Uh, yes, she *is* a Christian, actually. A very intelligent one, too. She reads St. Augustine for *fun*, mother. ...Yes, she has the read the Bible *many* times, almost as many as me. ...Mother, I am *not* being angry, I am just a little irritated that you still insist on majoring in the minors, even when I'm 27 years old!"

Charles saw his Aunt Brenda making a slashing motion with her hand, and shaking her head. She was standing across from him in the kitchen.

"Look, mother," said Charles, "I've gotta go. Brenda needs help cleaning up after dinner. ...Uh-huh. Love you too, mum."
Click.
Charles walked over to Brenda, shaking his head.
Brenda: "Well, I think Letty sounds like a real *peach*, Charlie."
"Thanks, Brenda."

A month after the day known as "Black Friday" (where Charlie gave Tony the what-for... in Cantonese, on a specific, exact date which I decline to disclose), Charles Irish finally got invited to eat dinner with Letty and her parents. It was a wonderful meal.

Letty and Irish sat across from Mr. and Mrs. Lung.

"Um... Irish," said Jessica Lung very sweetly, "what do you hope to do for a career after college?"

"It's a great question, ma'am," said Charlie. They were eating a pasta dish. Charles Irish loved pasta. "After I get my degree in Digital Marketing, I was hoping to find gainful employment as a salesman, to get job experience, and maybe use that as a stepping zone for a corporate role."

Tony Lung spoke for the first time during the meal.

"You should not be a salesman," he said flatly.

Everyone stared at Tony. Irish noted Letty wearing a poker-face, in his peripheral vision.

"No," said Tony Lung. "That would be wasting your potential. For that matter, so would studying Digital Marketing. I know about that program. The man who runs it is a hack."

Tony kept eating. He was enjoying his dinner.

About about six weeks passed by.

Tony and Charles took a long walk together on the afternoon of Thanksgiving. They'd all just had a big meal with the extended Lung family. Charles Irish was a regular guest at the Lung household by now, and a *de facto* guest of honor at this Thanksgiving dinner.

"I don't like being called 'Fang,'" said Tony, very patiently, "because I share that name with my Uncle in Hong Kong. That relative of mine is constantly asking me for money. But I always take his calls, in order to be respectful to an older relative whom I spent a lot of time with as a boy."

Charles Irish nodded. "I apologize for what I said on... 'Black Friday.' In Cantonese. I was presumptuous. Sir."

"It's fine," said Tony, shaking his head. "My daughter needs someone to solve her problems when I am not around. You... I think you can do that. If you're not scared off by either of us."

Irish chose his words carefully. They were the right words. "I'm not scared of either of you," said Irish. "I profoundly love and respect your whole family. Sir."

Tony Lung nodded, and smiled. "I understand that, Irish. Absolutely."

"Have a great summer, guys!" said the professor (he was the program chair of the Digital Marketing program) as Irish left the classroom.

Thanks, thought Irish. *Because my Spring was miserable.*

"Hey, Charlie!" said Letty. She had been waiting for him in the hallway. "Cokes?"

She knew that look. Another one of his dark moods.

"Something wrong, Irish?" said Letty.

Irish shook his head, and grasped Letty's right with his left. She took it.

"Let's talk at the green space we like," he said.

> *Side Note: Charlie was a sick man for a while.*
> *He got better. Mostly. A lot of the conflict between him*
> *and his parents was over how much of how he*
> *acted day-by-day was Charlie-being-sick*
> *versus Charlie-being-Charlie. Charlie Irish is*
> *exceptionally high-functioning, to use technically*
> *outdated jargon. Not every former psych ward patient*
> *can be like Charlie. There is only one* Irish.
> *Please keep that in mind, dear reader. ;-)*
> -Letty

Tony and Irish were sitting on the back porch of the Lung family's house. The Lung family lived in a very nice home in Sammamish. It was the morning after the Fourth of July.

"Hm. Automotive technology?" said Tony. "At Renton Tech?"

"Yeah," said Irish. "Marketing is… junk. I won't use stronger language than that. It's junk. Voodoo. Nonsense. I want to go to college to learn something useful, not learn how to be something I am not. Sir."

Tony smiled, and patted Irish on the shoulder.

"You are finally talking sense, my young friend," said Tony.

3 Years Later:

"Your boyfriend is an *auto mechanic?*" said Brooklyn at the grad party. Letty's grad party. Brooklyn had dropped out of Harvard Law after one year and, at the moment, was living with her parents in Snoqualmie. Letty's mom had invited her to the party.

"He's the best one at the shop," said Letty proudly. She'd had some healthy weight gain recently.

Charles Irish came in the back door. Running late.

"Hey, Lung," said Irish, "sorry, meant to be here earlier. Traffic coming up from Kent was a nightmare." Irish walked past an open-mouthed Brooklyn. Irish was wearing a blazer, slacks, and shiny shoes. And a tie. His hair looked great. He had new glasses. He'd changed into these clothes at work, in the bathroom, before coming to the party.

Irish gave Letty a quick peck on the cheek as he walked by, heading for the drink table.

Brooklyn turned to Letty. "Letty," she said, not-quite-whispering, "where did you find that, and where can I get one?"

Letty grinned, and said, "Not telling."

Irish and Letty were walking back to Irish's car from a performance of *Wicked* downtown. They were talking about the play, deep in conversation, when Irish stopped walking suddenly. He looked up, staring into the distance, at a large billboard advertising for the U.S. Army. It had some kind of recruitment slogan on it.

Letty saw where his eyes went. She also saw where his mind and heart were going.

But she had total control of his body.

"You don't have to become your dad, Irish," said Letty softly.

"You don't even have to become *my* dad! I like you for being you! Don't think that you have to be anyone else!"

Irish nodded, and put an arm around Letty. They walked back to where he had parked the car he'd driven there. It was a 2010 Toyota Camry. Colored black.

Letty and Irish were having dinner with Irish's parents. After being serious significant others for almost four years.

It wasn't going well.

"So, I'm just trying to get this straight," said Mrs. Irish. Mr. Irish was at the head of the table, saying nothing. "*What* did you study in college, um... Betty?"

"My name is *Letty*," said Letty, extremely patiently, "and I graduated with a four-year B.A.S. degree in Applied Accounting, and am currently working in an entry-level role at a business owned by my dad's old friend. My *dad* is a lawyer for a firm specializing in *securities fraud*. He sues *white-collar criminals* who haven't been caught by *the authorities*."

Charles was pretending to enjoy the meal.

Mrs. Irish scrunched up her face. She was 62 years old. A functioning, responsible adult, with a job. As was Mr. Irish.

"I don't like your attitude, little missy," she said crossly. "What are you making my son do to support you, again?"

Letty really, really wanted to summon her best smart-mouth routine. But Irish grasped her hand gently under the table.

Irish and Letty went back to the park where they had their first date. It was a dusky evening in June.

"I wish I didn't have to ask this, but..." Letty shook her head. "Your parents are devout, practicing, Christians in the broader

Evangelical-slash-Fundamentalist strain. Why…" She looked up at Irish. They were sitting in the back of the bed of his truck. He had two cars by now. And a rental house. Tony helped pay for utilities.

"Why are they kind of mean and jerky?" supplied Irish. "Despite knowing a lot about how… *non-jerky* and *non-mean* Jesus Christ was?"

Letty nodded. "Yeah," she said. Quietly.

Charles Irish sighed. "I don't know why my parents do what they do," he said. He reached into his jacket coat. He'd wanted to wait and do something special before he did this. He'd talked to Tony and Jessica already. *It's time*, he thought.

"But I know why *I* am doing *this*," he said, pulling out the ring. "Right now."

Letty jumped in her spot. "Charlie?" she said quietly, covering up her mouth with both hands.

"Letty Lung. Marry me."

Charlie and his dad were sitting in the front yard of Charles Irish's new house. It was a good, modest, house. The housing market in King County had improved significantly. Irish could never have afforded a home at 25, but at 35? Cake.

"So, yeah, I guess it's working out *now*," said Doug Irish, "but what about in a few years, when some kids come along? How much money do you even have in the bank? Have you thought about it? At all?"

Irish had spent many car rides with his dad, as a teenager, listening to his father complain about how badly the family business was doing. Irish had also taught himself accounting, knew a lot about business law, and unlike his father, had never had any significant consumer debt.

Charles Irish, as a teenager, was just kind of irritated that Dad always took it for granted that he was smarter than his son about *pretty much everything* because Charles Irish was... just little Chuckie. The poor, scared, chubby kid with acne who was obsessed with comic books. *Psh. What does little Chuckie know about that stuff?*

Little Chuckie was gone.

Charles Irish was doing just fine. Better than Doug Irish was at the same age, really.

Irish (kind of) wanted to say: *Dad, I have never had any debt whatsoever until I took out this home loan. I will most likely pay it off on time. Aren't you and mom still paying off a home loan on your house, when you got your mortgage, in like, 1991? I'm sorry, father, but I don't really respect your opinion on money.*

But he did not say that. Not anything close to that.

Remember: He wasn't Little Chuckie anymore. Ten or fifteen years ago, Little Chuckie would have whipped out a smart-mouth almost as potent that of as a certain Miss Lung.

But Charles Irish was there, in that lawn chair. Not Little Chuckie.

Irish said: "I'm taking care of it. Don't worry. Things will be fine, Dad."

Doug Irish said nothing.

"Nice day out," said Doug.

Doug and Kathy Irish moved into a mother-in-law house on Irish's property the same year. They changed their minds about Letty after tasting her cooking for the first time.

"Okay, Charles, supervisor numero-uno! How'd you like to go

to that conference in SLC next month?"

"A promotion *and* a raise? And you can do other work remotely? That's great, Irish!"

"Yes, of course, Charles, that is an *excellent* stock to buy. Here, let's go look at the stats…"

"And if it's a boy, we'll name him Raymond. After my uncle."

"Hi, Brooklyn! Yes, of course we'll come to your wedding! Thanks for calling! I'm so happy for you and Tristan! He sounds so sweet!"

"Hm. Fang? Yes, I'm alone, *and* I'm speaking Chinese… when are we talking to our attorney again about our Last Will and Testament? …Yes, I'm alone!"

"Hello, gentlemen of the board, and welcome. I proudly present Letty Irish, our top analyst. Mrs. Irish will now give the presentation on the finer points of the coming merger. Alright. Ahem. Take it away, Letty."

"Irish… why don't you just go write that Great American Novel already? Just for kicks? I'd read it... Whoa! Whoa! Hey hey, be good! Be good! Hey- Oomfth... Mmm... Mmm..."

* * *

Yeah, so, that's how Charles Irish became a famous writer. Yeah. True story. Yup.

-Letty Irish (nee Lung)

Afterword

There was a commercial for *The Dark Knight Rises* playing on a TV in the rec room of the psych ward I was in on the day I left. I was almost seventeen years old at the time.

I suffer from mental illness. I've been living with psychosis for the better part of 15 years, as of this writing. My medical providers currently think that, whatever I've got, it might be classifiable as Bipolar II.

The sequencing of the contents of *Songbird!* is meant to trace my evolution as a writer, from naivete to... the beginning of maturity. I personally trace a general arc of me consciously trying to be poetic (Part 1), followed by my attempts to get out of my shell and get my work in front of an audience (Part 2), before settling into my current era, where I just write the best darn poems and stories I can, and if I like them, that's just fine, thanks (Part 3).

The actual Kenny G track *Songbird* does not accidentally share a title with this book. I was first introduced to that track when I was, like, 11. It was part of a slapstick punchline in the film *Cars*. I first saw it on DVD, not in theaters (I think). Great movie. I haven't seen the sequels.

A lot of my writing, whether my poetry or my stories, has to do with themes of family, community, and spirituality. I believe I have an unlikely affinity for the filmography of M. Night Shyamalan because we share a predilection for those themes. Mr. Shyamalan, if you are reading this, I have a message for you: You're awesome. I even found some things to like about *The Last Airbender*. You go get 'em, brother.

Some people think that some of my later, recent stories are "cinematic" and like "screenplays." Maybe they are. They were all originally conceived at short stories, but I do admit to picturing them as short films in my head as I wrote them. I consider these later stories, found in Part 3, to be some of my best work. I really like the poems in that section the best, too.

I do take a lot of inspiration from outside of literature. A lot of authors like to list their biggest inspirations in their bios, or how they have "always wanted to be a writer" or something.

What are *my* inspirations? *Who* are my inspirations?

My father. My mother. My sisters. My Grandma and my late Grandpa Pat. My aunts, my uncles, my cousins. My best friend, my friends, my acquaintances, colleagues, mentors, and teachers. That Vietnamese teenager who helps sell sandwiches at that deli up the street, who wears braces and smiles really big when I give her a nice cash tip.

I am inspired by people.

Most of the *authors* who inspire me are now dead.

The ones who are still around are people I would love to grab lunch with someday.

Messrs. Dixon, Colfer, Card? Look me up sometime. On Google.

Cheers, mates.

Levi Sweeney
Bryn Mawr-Skyway, May 2025

About the Author

Levi Sweeney is a lifelong Seattleite. He has been a janitor, a landscaper, a Sunday School teacher, a psych ward patient, a garbage boy, a dishwasher, a community college drop-out, a cashier, a teller, a GOP activist in Seattle, a college radio producer (in that order), and now he is trying to be a writer. His biggest accomplishments include surviving a car accident, converting to Catholicism at 23, and never once getting sued or arrested. He used to think his life was boring. He has recently changed his mind.